from Clara Jackson
for KSU Jun. Coll.

D1029291

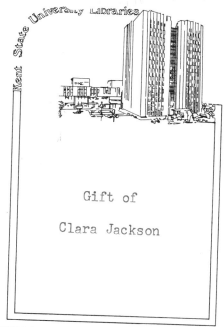

Honey in the Rock

Honey in the Rock

by

Doris Kirkpatrick

Elsevier/Nelson Books
New York

No character in this book is intended to represent any actual person; all the incidents of the story are entirely fictional in nature.

Library of Congress Cataloging in Publication Data

Kirkpatrick, Doris.
  Honey in the rock.

  SUMMARY: During the autumn of 1936, a 16-year-old girl begins to see signs that life in her small village in Vermont is drastically changing.
  [1. Vermont—Fiction] I. Title.
PZ7.K6353Ho   [Fic]   79–4094
ISBN 0–525–66643–5

Published in the United States by Elsevier / Nelson Books, a division of Elsevier-Dutton Publishing Company, Inc., New York. Published simultaneously in Don Mills, Ontario, by Thomas Nelson and Sons [Canada] Limited.

Printed in the U.S.A.   First Edition

10 9 8 7 6 5 4 3 2 1

Honey
in the Rock

1.

JAN HAD SOMETHING on his mind, Linny knew. All the way up Chase Hill on their way home from high school, he had been kicking at pebbles. Linny stopped and faced him. She drew her slim body up to its full height, determined to find out what was wrong. "Jan, what's bothering you?" she demanded.

They were both sixteen, but Jan was a head taller than Linny. He was broad-shouldered and solidly built. His deep-set black eyes looked down at her half embarrassed, half defiant. "I've got news you won't like," he said reluctantly.

His eyes followed the track of afternoon June sun that ribboned the trunks of the great maples towering on both sides of the road. How could he make her understand?

"As soon as school is out this summer I'm going to work for the Power Company." He waited for her reaction, which he knew would be stormy.

Linny flared up like a rocket. Her hazel eyes sparked. "The Power Company! Jan Brokowski, how could you!"

Even when she was angry she was pretty, Jan thought. Her cheeks got flushed, and her chin set itself stubbornly. But he wished she'd get over her fear of the Power Company.

"Water doesn't run uphill," he said patiently. "The

1

Power Company won't be extending the reservoir up on Chase Hill to your place."

Linny shook her shoulder-length brown hair in exasperation. "Grandma is worried. The pasture south of the house fronts on the river. The Power Company will want the Chase place too. Look at all the people in the village who have lost their homes already!"

"They got spot cash for them," Jan said stubbornly. "And when the dam is finished, they'll be glad enough to have the power. Linny, it's 1936, not 1890. Up here in Sadawga Springs you'd never know it. Folks are still living in the horse-and-buggy age."

Although Linny was slim and small-boned, Jan knew that her appearance of delicacy was deceptive. She had the endurance of a Shetland pony and she would not give up.

Linny hesitated. Then, swallowing her wrath, she tried another approach. "Your ma won't like it," she said, substituting guile for anger. She knew his mother was always at him to give up school and manage the farm, which was about a mile outside the village.

"Ma doesn't need me the way she did," he said as if he were brushing a cobweb out of his way. "When the dam is finished and power comes on we can get a milking machine and milk thirty cows in an hour."

After all, Poles clung to the land as stubbornly as Vermonters, Linny thought. "Since your father died your mother has slaved and sacrificed to build up a good farm," she said. "She'll want you to carry on."

"I've got my own life to live." A shade of annoyance crept into Jan's voice. "Besides, she'll be glad enough for my wages."

Linny knew that it had been a struggle for Jan's mother. The villagers had not welcomed the coming of two or three Polish families. Even Jan had not been spared. Linny would never forget his first day at school in the second grade when his folks had moved to Sadawga Springs from a mining town in Pennsylvania. Jan had been friendly and outgoing from the start, but the whole class had cold-shouldered him. It had been no fun being a stranger in a strange school. But Linny had given him an apple from her lunch box, and they had been friends ever since. Now Jan was the most popular boy in his class, and the smartest too.

"Jan, you ought to be going away to college next year," she said, her voice soft and appealing. "You could get a scholarship. You could study to be a teacher or doctor. But if you work for the Power Company . . ." Her voice trailed off. It wouldn't be for just the summer. He'd get attached to the Power Company. He was so bright he'd get ahead. Someday he might even be buying up other folks' property somewhere, the way the company was doing now in Sadawga Springs.

Jan pushed back his black hair, which was always falling into his eyes. "I'd go crazy shut up in a schoolroom all my life, and I don't give a snap of my fingers for medicine. I like machinery."

"You want to be a bolt in a machine instead of a man," Linny said bitterly.

His patience vanished. "What have you got against the Power Company?" he exploded. "Look what it's going to do for Sadawga Springs—cut taxes, bring in modern improvements, new roads, a new schoolhouse. Summer people will flock here, and real estate will go sky high."

"Sure," she said in scorn, "summer people who run around to auctions, buying up antiques, and who let their orchards go to seed. People like that New York banker who's afraid to get his hands dirty and lets his pastures grow up to forest."

"So what?" Jan broke in, his voice thick with irritation. "All Vermont's rocky farmland is good for is scenery."

The ground was damp underfoot, and Linny shivered as the chill crept through the thin soles of her shoes and up her ankles.

"You can't reason with prejudice," Jan said, abandoning hope of coming to an understanding.

Abruptly Linny turned and began to stumble up the hill.

She felt his hand on her arm, pulling her back. His breath was warm on her cheek. "Linny," he said softly, "no matter what Ma says, I'm going back to finish high school. After I graduate I'll need a job. Where are there jobs today with thirteen million out of work? In the cities men are selling apples in the streets. I've got to look ahead. I'm lucky to have a chance like this, and there's a future in the Power Company."

The sun had gone under a cloud. The outline of his face blurred as her eyes misted over. He seemed far away and somehow lost to her. There was a low rumble in the northwest. A flash of lightning streaked down in the pasture.

"It's going to shower hard, Jan. Go back," she said. She snatched her strapped schoolbooks from his hand and sped off swift as a deer. She knew he was standing there staring after her, but she did not turn around and wave.

She had a dismal feeling that Jan would never understand about the Chase place. Generations of Chases had lived there since the Revolution. The old house didn't belong to Grandma and Grandpa. *They* belonged to the house. She had learned that at an early age.

She remembered again the swift changes that had come when she was six years old. One day she had had two loving, laughing parents, and the next day they had been lost to her in a car crash on an icy road in Boston. Uncle Nat had taken charge. "Linny, you've got to be a brave girl now," he had said. But his words had failed to reach her. Lost in a vast tract of nothingness, she made no protest that winter day when Uncle Nat put her on the train for Vermont, her ticket pinned to her coat.

In silence she had followed the conductor when he helped her change to the narrow-gauge railway at Hoosac Tunnel. As the small train rocked around the mountains she had looked down into the cavernous depths below and felt alone in a wide world of strangeness.

The conductor had put her off at Sadawga Springs station, where Grandpa met her with his sleigh. Coarse black fur had tickled her nose as the tall figure bent down over her and grasped her bag, which the conductor had dropped on the snowy ground. She blinked and peered up into her grandpa's face. Under his black fur cap his cheeks were as red as apples. His long, lean face was rough as the bark of a tree. He looked rooted, too, like a tree, and she wanted to catch hold of his big mitten.

"Howdy," he said, and swung her up into the sleigh as if she were a feather. Then he climbed in beside her and tucked a buffalo robe around her legs. "Giddap, Fan," he said, picking up the reins.

The sleigh bells jingled merrily as Fan trotted along. Deep-purple hills loomed on both sides of the road. Suddenly Linny saw chimney smoke circling up on the thick blue of the sky. She sat up and pushed back the robe to see better.

The valley lay before them, a snowy hollow that some giant hand had scooped out of the mountains. "Well," Grandpa said, "here's Sadawga Springs."

Across the road snow had drifted up the steep steps

of a green-shuttered church, and snow plugged the entrance of the town hall next door. Snow banked the silent houses grouped in the village. Not a door opened, not a face appeared at a window. In the ghostly whiteness and stillness the only sound was the squeak of the sleigh runners and the shrill piping of the wind.

Grandpa had pulled up in front of an unpainted building with a crooked signboard that clattered in the wind. Through the frosty windows Linny glimpsed rubber boots toppled against blue jeans and dingy soap. "Been a Butterfield in the general store for four generations," Grandpa offered in explanation.

He creaked down out of the sleigh and lifted Linny out, and she followed him into the store. As he opened the door the tinkle of a little bell startled Linny. She sniffed the mingled odor of pickles, kerosine, and spices. Some men were grouped around a potbellied stove in which a fire crackled. Linny moved close to Grandpa's coat, and when he headed for a corner filled with mailboxes, she was at his heels. He twirled a dial and took out a newspaper, the *Deerfield Valley Times*. "Your grandma likes to know what's goin' on," he said.

Thrusting the paper in his pocket, he stepped up to the counter and laid down a coin. "Howdy, John," he said. "A dime's worth of chocolate creams. This here's Linny Storrs, my granddaughter come to live with us."

The lanky figure behind the counter handed Grandpa a striped paper bag and laid down a chocolate in front of Linny. "Welcome to Sadawga Springs," he said.

A giant of a man disentangled himself from the knot of men at the stove and rose to his feet. "I'm Mose Shawn, stage driver," he said to Linny, burrowing in his pocket. "Have a stick of gum."

Cautiously Linny edged forward and accepted the gum, mumbling her thanks. Then, with the chocolate clutched in one hand and the gum in the other, she followed Grandpa out of the store. As she nibbled on the chocolate, the tightness inside her began to loosen up.

In the sleigh again, Grandpa gave Fan her head as they began to climb up toward the snow-covered mountains. As they passed a latticed springhouse that sheltered an iron pump, Grandpa said, "That's Sadawga Spring. It pumps up iron water. Folks come from miles around to take the water cure."

On a knoll above the springhouse crouched a squat box of a building with a large bell in a tower on the roof. "That's the district schoolhouse where you'll go to school," Grandpa said.

Linny found her voice. "Do I *have* to go to school?" she mourned.

Grandpa didn't argue the matter. "Giddap, Fan," he said. At a fork in the road another road branched off up another hill seemingly straight into the sky. "Chase Hill," Grandpa said.

He pulled Fan to a stop in front of a square white house that was connected to a large barn by an arched shed. A voice called, "Uncle Newt!" Then a door was flung open and a woman in rubber boots with a man's coat thrown over her shoulders plowed through the snow toward them. She was panting when she pulled up at the sleigh, her cheeks red with cold, her eyes bright. Linny looked at the woman curiously. She wasn't as pretty as her mother had been, with her chestnut hair drawn back smoothly from her face, but she was tall and strong-looking. She smiled and tiny lines crinkled around her mouth.

"So this is Linny," she said in a deep, husky voice, putting her hand on the dashboard. Her warm, steady eyes rested on Linny. "I'm your cousin, Martha Chase, though most folks call me Mart. Your grandma is my pa's sister, so that makes us second cousins."

She looked up at the hill rising stark and steep into the sky. "I just wanted you to know you had kin near you. When you are settled on the hill you come down and see us."

Linny gulped and stared at the strong fingers on the dashboard reddening with cold. She tried to speak, but the words wouldn't come out.

After a few words with Mart Grandpa lifted the reins and they plunged on through the snow. Linny turned her head to watch as Mart stomped back to the house through the snow.

As they climbed the last rise of the hill, the road ahead seemed to get darker, and the sky to bear down upon them. The wind burned and stung Linny's cheeks. Her eyelids felt pasted back with cold. Grandpa sat like a block of ice, and the only sound was Fan's breath coming gustily from her nostrils.

When they reached the top Linny stared out at the barren whiteness stretching off to the distant hills. A small two-story house topped by two chimneys clung to the snowy ground. Snow stuck to its paintless, weathered clapboards, to its long, low roof, and to its narrow windows. Overhead towered a giant maple, a strong wind rattling through its skeleton arms.

Grandpa swung Linny down out of the sleigh and shoved her across the threshold as if she had been a sawdust doll. "Well, here ye be," he said.

She had a confused sense of a low-ceilinged room with faded wallpaper, wide floorboards spotted with rag rugs, and straight-back, rush-bottomed chairs. At one end of the room a round table covered with a red-checked tablecloth was set for supper. Between two windows bright with geraniums, a comfortable couch looked inviting. A Franklin stove gave off heat.

Linny's glance winged up to a huge figure who stood listening to a box telephone on the wall, one great hand clamped over the mouthpiece. When she saw Linny she hung up the receiver and made her way across the floor with the aid of a cane. Fierce eyebrows jutted from her heavy face. Long black hairs sprouted from her upper lip and her chin.

"Whatcha standin' there for like a chicken that's lost its tail! Git them things off, young'un, afore you freeze to the floor. I'm too old and lame with the rheumatiz to be a waitin' on you."

As Linny pulled off her coat and boots Grandma towered over her. Her bright eyes swept over Linny from head to foot, not missing her skinny elbows and knees. "Don't look much like your ma . . . or your pa either . . . no, sirree," she snorted.

Grandma dropped down on a haircloth sofa flanked by a marble-topped table. Grandpa dug in his pocket and dropped the striped paper bag into Grandma's lap. "Here's somewhat to sweeten you up, Kit," he said, with a wink at Linny.

"Linny, have a chocolate cream," Grandma said. She took one chocolate out and squashed it in her strong teeth.

"She'll talk your ear off," Grandpa warned Linny.

"Fiddlesticks, it ain't every day a Chase comes home," Grandma said, taking another chocolate.

Linny was confused. "I'm not a Chase," she said timidly. "My name is Linda Storrs."

"Bless you, child," Grandma boomed out. "Betsy Chase, my ma, was your great-grandmother. I was born Calista Chase in this house. My ma was Betsy Tainter before she married Nathan Chase and come to this house as a bride." She picked up a cherry-wood box from the marble-topped table and held it in her lap. Opening up the box, she took out a brooch and handed it to Linny. "My pa, Nathan Chase, had my ma's picture a-wearin' her wedding dress painted on this brooch by a travelin' painter feller. Got a livin' look to her, ain't she?"

Linny stared curiously at the still face that looked back at her in calm acceptance. Smooth hair, parted in the middle, was drawn down to end in stiff little curls that brushed the lace collar. The eyes, large and dark and full of fire, seemed to speak.

"Linny, look at me," Grandma demanded. "If you ain't the spittin' image of my ma Betsy Chase!"

The sun sifted yellow dust on the wide floorboards. Linny crept close to the sofa, looking at the high color flooding Grandma's cheeks. One great arm stole around her. From the doorway Grandpa's winter-sky eyes sparkled down at her. She clutched the brooch tight in her hand and leaned against Grandma's knee.

"My, ain't you a little mite," Grandma clucked. "We got to fatten you up good."

Stuffed with Grandma's griddle cakes, pies, doughnuts, and thick cream in the years that followed, Linny put on weight. But she always remained slim. Grandpa made her a set of snowshoes and taught her how to use them, so even in winter, Linny tramped uphill and down over pasture, meadow, and lane, seeing the deepening winter blue of the skies, the green of firs against the snow, and the purple shadows on the hills. Every day she fed bread crumbs to the chickadees clustered in the yard. When she came in, cheeks burning with cold, eyes sun-blinded by the sparkling snow crust, she warmed herself in front of the Franklin stove, chewed on hard, sweet Baldwins and munched the hazelnuts Grandpa cracked for her on a turned-up flatiron. As each snowbound day slid into the next, an endless chain marching with a slow, unhurried tread, Linny came to feel that she had never known and never would know any other kind of life.

Why couldn't things stay the way they had always been? A drop of rain splashed down on Linny's nose, and she quickened her steps up the hill. Black thunderheads had piled up over the tops of the mountains, and it was dark as a cat's pocket. As she turned in the yard the small house crouched low against the ground seemed to be shrouded in mist as if it were being spirited away.

Through the dimness Linny caught a glimpse of a long, low car, and fear spread through her with icy fingers. Had it come at last? Swiftly she passed the front of the house, ran around to the back, and pushed open the kitchen door.

The kitchen was warm. Fire crackled in the black cookstove, from which issued the fragrant smell of beans baking. It seemed peaceful enough. Through the doorway came the sound of Grandma's loud voice plunging on a mile a minute.

The tall figure of Grandpa came through the kitchen doorway from the barn. He was carrying an empty milk pail, which he set down in the wooden sink and then rinsed with spring water from a barrel next to the sink. "Kit's been goin' on like that for nigh on an hour. Talks the handle off a pump," he chuckled.

"Is he from the Power Company?" Linny asked fearfully.

"I reckon," Grandpa said dryly. "But so far he hasn't been able to get a word in edgewise."

Linny stationed herself at the edge of the doorway where she couldn't be seen and listened. It was unthinkable that Grandma would sell the Chase place to the Power Company!

2

IN THE KITCHEN Linny peered around the corner of the doorjamb. Grandma was sitting on the haircloth sofa, her great knees spread apart like the trunks of twin oaks. The stranger sat in the Windsor rocker, his hat on his knees. His face was pink and clean shaven. He opened his mouth to speak, but Grandma was ahead of him. For a moment Linny almost felt a stir of pity for him. He didn't know what he was up against.

"We ain't got any land up here on the hill you would be wantin'," Grandma thundered.

"It's true your house would not be covered by the reservoir, but we need your place for a watershed," he said. "We plan to set out young pines along the shore to hold down the earth."

"So," Grandma muttered, her face stony as the side of a cliff.

His smile was nailed on tight. "Now look here, Mrs. Storrs," he said, easy as if they were old friends, "we want you to know, and we want the community to know, that we don't do business in a high-handed way. We were glad to hear about the town meeting tonight. The only way is to get everybody together and talk matters over with fair play and justice for everyone, without recourse to law. We want folks satisfied."

Lines of grim humor stretched down the corners of

Grandma's mouth. "Guess you ain't never been to a town meeting, mister. Trouble with Yanks is they ain't logical. A matter has got to hit 'em just so, or it don't hit 'em at all."

His cheeks flushed and his smooth forehead wrinkled. "But surely they can't be blind to their own self-interest," he said. "Now take the matter of Mr. Chase's property at the foot of Chase Hill. He's not dependent on the farm, is he? I understand he makes his living at his mill. There's not much value to that acreage. There's no timber on it. It's poor pasture land."

"Yep," Grandma said. She reached in her apron pocket, popped a wad of spruce gum into her mouth, and chewed lustily.

The man breathed a sigh of relief. "With the generous cash payment we are willing to make him, he could build a new modern house with all conveniences on any spot he liked."

"What you want Truman's land for?" Grandma shot at him.

His eyes lighted up as if he were seeing visions. "Someday you'll see a reservoir at the foot of the hill that will stretch back twelve miles, all the way to Wilmington. We want to buy up all land on either side of the Deerfield River, to set out to pines for a watershed."

Did that mean Mart's house would be under water? Linny listened in shocked disbelief, waiting for Grandma to pounce on the man.

But Grandma scowled at a fly on the windowpane. "Well, it ain't just the house, mister. Truman don't want to see no city ways creepin' up into these here mountains. He never was forward looking. The old ways was always good enough for him."

The stranger crossed his legs and regarded the cuffs

of his trousers. "But isn't that selfish prejudice? If everybody felt that way, there'd be no progress."

What ailed Grandma? She sat motionless on the sofa, like a great boulder that had come to rest. Linny couldn't believe her ears when she heard Grandma say, "Maybe so. I studied it over in my mind some. I was brung up in the hoss-and-buggy age, but I got nothin' agin automobiles. As for radios, I wouldn't mind havin' one of them contraptions. I like to know what's goin' on."

The stranger chuckled. "Mrs. Storrs, you shall have anything you like if you lend us your support. This dam is the business of the whole community. It will mean electric power and the machines that go with power. It will create work for hundreds of people, bring business to Sadawga Springs and more summer people."

"I've heard that when machines come into a place and the people that control 'em, there's times when the machines stop and folks git laid off. There ain't no progress in Sadawga Springs, but there ain't nobody never gone hungry, neither."

The stranger shrugged his shoulders. "The machine age has its problems, of course. The Depression has hit us hard. But there's no turning back. We've got to go forward."

Grandma stared out at the road that disappeared into the maples. "What we got here on Chase Hill is something you don't likely understand. We ain't forgettin' how the first Nathan Chase and his wife Abigail come up from Connecticut before the Revolution pulling their goods on a handsled. This was wild country then: snow and Indians and unbroken ground."

In the kitchen Linny felt Grandpa brush by her. "Kit's off and goin' it now," he said, and went into the living room. "Howdy, stranger," he mumbled as he sat down in a straight chair and pulled his pipe out of his pocket as if he were settling down for a long stay.

The stranger hardly noticed Grandpa. His eyes were on Grandma as she pointed. "See that portrait hangin' over the cherry table? That's my ma, Betsy Chase. Delicate-like for a farm woman, ain't she? I recall how she'd bleach her hands with buttermilk after a work day in the fields. And she wore lace mitts to the end of her days."

Grandma paused for breath and then went on. "My pa brung her to this house as a bride, and her folks was fit to be tied. Nate Chase was nothing but a backwoods farmer. He wa'n't good enough for the daughter of Deliverance Tainter."

Grandma chuckled. "Young man, hand me that album on the marble-top table."

Linny knew well what the stranger was in for.

Grandma flipped over the stiff pages. "See there. Nathan Chase and Betsy. That dress was four yards round, white with blue bows in the skirt and a tight bodice that buttoned down the front. Her pa, Deliverance Tainter—a rapscallion he was, but money stuck to his fingers—he sent clear to Boston for that dress, and she was married in it down at the old Brick House at the end of the pasture lane."

A great sigh bumbled up out of Grandma, like the cough of a steam engine. Crisply she turned a page. "There's my pa the year he died from consumption. Only thirty-three he was, and left three children: Nathan, who drowned in Lake Sadawga as a boy, Truman, and me."

The stranger moved restlessly, as if he would like to be up and away. But there was no stopping Grandma. "Them was hard times for Betsy, but she stuck to the land. How she fed us, I dunno. A little thing she was, not over five feet. But she plowed like a man, rode the hayrack, milked and planted. Always kept somethin' in our stomachs. She brewed coffee out of parched corn and made a pair of shoes for Truman out of an old piece of carpeting."

"I'm sure this is all very interesting, but I really must be going," the stranger said quickly, trying to get a word in edgewise.

But he was no match for Grandma. "Here's my brother Truman's wife Jen, what's dead now. She had a rough time of it up on Freezin' Hole Mountain, with only bears and wildcats for company. Their daughter Martha was born up on Freezin' Hole in the dead of winter. After Truman hurt his right leg when a tree fell on it, they moved down to the village at the foot of Chase Hill."

"Mart's a good daughter to that skinflint pa of hers," Grandma went on. "Robert, her brother, is a scallywag—never do nothin' for nobody. He lit out and become a newspaper man, traipsin' all over foreign parts. But Mart wouldn't leave her pa to wash his own floors. Thirty years old she was when she married her cousin Jared Chase from Jacksonville. A sight younger'n Mart, Jared was, and no hand for farmin' steady. How the tongues wagged. Let 'em wag, I say."

Grandma snorted and flipped a page. "I swan! Here's me before I was married. Was I homely! Chunky as a bag of meal and hair straight as a string. There wa'n't a boy in town I couldn't smack down with one hand."

"Not to mention the use you could put your tongue to," Grandpa added dryly.

Grandma bolted on. "Here's when I was married. Folks had give me up for an old maid. I met Newton Storrs when we was fightin' a forest fire, both of us black from head to foot. He come from up Wilmington way, and I says to him when he ask for my hand, 'I'll never set foot from the Nathan Chase place, but if you can put up with me you can hang your hat here as long as you're a mind to.' "

"Well, it's been hangin' here nigh onto fifty years." Grandpa's pipe had gone out. He struck a match on the seat of his blue jeans and lit his pipe again.

"So you see, stranger, there's been a lot of livin' in this old house, and we don't aim to part with it." Grandma threw back her head and roared, "Linny, I know you're there in the kitchen. Bring in a plate of them beans and a cup of coffee."

The stranger raised a hand in protest, but when the fragrant, steaming plate of beans was offered him he did not refuse.

"You and I are on opposite sides of the fence," Grandma chortled, "but I dunno's that's any call to act like the heathen Chinee."

The stranger obviously enjoyed Grandma's beans. When he had finished eating and thanked her he drew out a card from his vest pocket and handed it to Grandma. The small card looked somehow ridiculous in Grandma's thick fingers.

"We'll talk things over at the town meeting, and maybe we'll hope to come to some amicable agreement," he said. "I'll be back."

As the door shut behind him Linny burst out, "Grandma, you treated him like company!"

Grandma got up from the sofa. "Crimus, how's a body to make up his mind about a thing until he knows all the outs and ins?" she roared.

She hobbled into the pantry, her long white petticoat swirling up over her boot tops as she leaned down and swung up a pint can of new maple syrup. She thumped it down on the shelf. "Linny, I want you should take this new syrup down to Truman before supper and find out if he's goin' to the town meeting tonight. Get a move on now. I want to know what's goin' on."

3

THE RAIN had stopped and it had turned colder. The wind licked Linny's face, and the freezing mud crackled under her feet as she trudged down the hill carrying the syrup can. Warming her cheek with her mitten, she wondered wearily if it was because of the stranger that Grandma was in such a fret about Uncle Truman.

When she opened Mart's kitchen door a gush of warmth rushed out to greet her. Half blind from the light, she could make out Uncle Truman sitting under the big white-shaded Rochester burner reading the *Deerfield Valley Times*. Mart's husband Jared was washing at the sink while Mart mashed potatoes at the stove.

"Something wrong?" Mart's potato masher paused in midair.

Linny handed her the syrup can. "Grandma sent you down some new syrup for supper. She says it's first run."

Mart pushed the potato dish to the back of the stove, wiped her hands on her apron, and took the can. She unscrewed the top and poured a golden stream into a glass pitcher. "My, first run," she said. "Nobody can make syrup as good as Uncle Newt." But Linny saw the question in her eyes.

"Uncle Truman." Linny lifted her voice, trying to penetrate the wall of the outspread newspaper. "Grandma wants to know if you are going to the town meeting tonight." She moved toward the stove and held one chilled foot up to the grate.

The newspaper was lowered. Uncle Truman's rugged red face turned toward her. "She does, eh?" He rubbed a hand over his grizzled chin. "Well, I aim to."

"She had a visitor this afternoon from the Power Company," Linny went on. "He wanted to buy the Chase house. But Grandma wouldn't sell."

"I heard he was in town," Truman said. "No good will come of it. As for Kit, she'll never part with the Chase homestead."

Mart's face looked troubled. She poured hot water into a brown earthen teapot. "Better take off your things, Linny, and warm up before you go back up the hill," she said.

Jared lifted his dripping face from the washbasin, and Mart threw him a towel. He rubbed his ears pink, then draped the towel over one shoulder. A lean arm shot out and caught Mart, and he planted a damp smacker on her cheek.

"Go 'long with you," Mart said, giving him a little shove.

Mart's cheeks were red as checkerberries, but otherwise she seemed to be her familiar serene and untroubled self, Linny thought. She moved reluctantly toward the door. "I've got to get back and help Grandma with the supper."

She had just laid her hand on the latch when the knock sounded, a short, smart rap. She flung open the door, and in the lamplight streaming through it stood a short, thick-set figure in an English tweed coat. It was the stranger. She hadn't seen or heard his car come.

"Good evening," he said in a pleasant voice. "Is Mr. Truman Chase at home?"

Mart leaned over Linny's shoulder. "Why, yes, he is," she said in her slow, rich voice. "Won't you come in?"

Linny knew she ought to go, but when the stranger stepped into the kitchen she drew back from the door into a shadowy corner by the stove, watching him take off his gray felt hat. Mart hung it on a hook on the wall, and Linny saw Jared stare at it hanging there beside their old caps.

The man began to unbutton his overcoat with the sure poise and calm of someone who knows he's on the right side.

Uncle Truman got up and motioned toward the rocker. "Have a seat, stranger."

The visitor sat down in the rocker and stretched out his legs comfortably. Linny noticed that he was wearing richly polished, stitched leather shoes and silk socks. He leaned back, in no hurry to state his errand.

A wary look came into Uncle Truman's eyes, and he carefully lowered himself into one of the straight kitchen chairs, his back tense and upright.

The stranger leaned forward, his hands with their well-manicured nails clasped loosely between his knees. "I won't beat around the bush any. I guess you know why I'm here."

Uncle Truman took out his pipe and lit it. "I can guess, but that don't mean I'm for it," he said.

"My name is Wells—Charles Wells." He took an engraved card from his pocket and handed it to Uncle Truman.

Uncle Truman's gaze flicked over the card, and he laid it down on the table.

Mart placed her hand on the back of Truman's chair, and he handed her the card. "This here stranger is from the Green Valley Power Company. They figger to put up a dam on the Deerfield River, and they're coming around trying to git their hands on folks' property."

"I was afraid of this," Mart murmured.

"Now," the stranger said in a soothing voice, "let's talk this over quietly. Think what it will mean to Sadawga Springs to have the largest earth dam in the country." He motioned toward the kerosine lamp on the table. "You farmers can have electric lights that come on at the push of a button."

Uncle Truman puffed on his pipe, his mouth clamped tight around the stem. "Up here in the woods we work by daylight and, come night, we go to bed," he said.

"You can have a modern electric stove"—the stranger nodded toward the wood range—"instead of that anachronism."

"That range was good enough for my wife, and it's good enough for my daughter," Truman muttered.

"And an electric refrigerator and a washing machine, to say nothing of a milking machine and separator," the man went on, "and all at rock-bottom price, six cents per kilowatt hour."

Jared scratched his head and eyed Mart. "Electricity can save a powerful lot of labor. Summer folks always want it," he said hesitantly.

The stranger seized the opening. "You mountain folk should have some of the advantages city people are accustomed to. Here they'll be, right at your door."

"It isn't always how good a thing is, it's what it costs," Mart murmured.

The stranger beamed. "No matter how you look at it, it's all velvet for you people. You get way above market prices for your property and you get the advantages of cheap power. And consider the taxes our company will pay. You will be the richest township in Vermont. You can have paved roads, a new schoolhouse, and a new town hall. Summer people will flock here. Workers will come in and bring business and settle down. Why, this will be the biggest boom this town has ever seen."

The frown on Mart's smooth forehead deepened. "It would mean a good many changes," she said in her slow voice.

"You can't stop the wind from blowing, Mart," Jared said, and there was an eager look in his eye.

Truman's head shot up. "There'll be changes all right," he growled. "If their plans go through they'll wipe out the railroad, the station, Sugar Hill Cemetery, and darn near one third of the village."

Linny gasped. She had a sudden vision of torrents of water pouring through the village, drowning roofs and chimneys from sight. She jumped to her feet and her elbow joggled the handle of the mashed-potato pan and set it spinning across the stove. Mart deftly caught the pan and set it up on the stove shelf. "There," she said, her voice steady, "nothing's happened yet."

The stranger leaned back in his chair and thrust a thumb in his vest. "Now there's no need to get upset," he said in a kindly voice. "Nice place you have here, Mr. Chase, if a bit old-fashioned. I don't blame you Vermonters for clinging to your homes. But you miss the real issue. After all, one house is as good as another. You can buy another farm, modernize it, and start over ahead of the game."

There was a steely glint in Truman's eye. "I ain't fixin' to start over," he said.

The stranger took out a clean white handkerchief and wiped the palms of his hands.

"Mr. Chase, let's look at this thing as a business proposition. This farm at the outside isn't worth more than four thousand dollars, and my company is pre-pared to make you the more-than-generous offer of ten thousand dollars. Think of that, ten thousand," he said impressively. "Put you on easy street."

Uncle Truman opened his gnarled old hands and regarded the thick fingers that had felled trees for fifty years. "I guess us Vermonters wouldn't feel at home on easy street," he said.

"Mr. Chase." The man's voice was slow and even. "Think how many years ago men plowed the earth with ox-drawn plows, harvested with the scythe, and threshed with a flail. Today you have the tractor, the harvester, and the thresher. Why, the cloth for the clothes you wear on your back was turned out by vast, power-driven spindles and looms. This is the age of machinery. The age of power. You can't escape it, even up here in the mountains. You're a century behind the times. The world is changing."

Uncle Truman struggled to his feet, his face a dull purplish red. Mart stood motionless. Linny held her breath, her eyes on Uncle Truman as he clumped to the stove, lifted the lid, and spat. The grim line of his brows curved over the snapping flames. His mouth was flint.

"Maybe so, stranger. But don't fergit our forefathers come up here into virgin wilderness because they had a hankerin' in their bellies to live under their own say-so. We aim to keep it that way."

He faced the stranger, a heavy, squat figure in woollen shirt and overalls, his face set like the granite pasture rock.

Mart handed the stranger his hat. "Sorry you have to go, mister," she said steadily.

The stranger sighed and then came to life. He sprang up out of his rocker with a burst of energy. "The Green Valley Power Company is an empire," he said. He settled his gray hat on his head and stood looking at them, a well-set-up, impressive figure with neither defeat nor disappointment written on his face. "We have over two thousand miles of wire carrying current to industries, farms, stores, and homes. We serve thousands of customers. We're an empire," he repeated, his voice charged with dark meaning. Linny almost thought she saw a look of pity in his eyes. "Well, you think it over," he said cheerfully. "I'll be back."

As the door closed behind him, there was dead silence in the kitchen. Linny looked from one still face to another. The crackling of the fire, the tick of the clock sounded loud and somehow ominous.

"I've worked up an appetite. I been chopping wood all day," Jared said, and stretched his legs under the table.

Mart took ham from the warming oven and set it in front of him in silence. She picked up the earthen teapot and poured him a cup of tea.

Uncle Truman took down his coat from a peg on the wall and put it on. "I ain't hungry. I'm walkin' up the hill with Linny to see Kit," he muttered.

Mart paused at the window, teapot in hand, and looked out at the dark rim of the mountains against the evening sky.

"Better take a lantern, Pa, to light you home," she said quietly.

4.

"LINNY, I WANT YOU to go down to the town meeting with your grandpa so's you can tell me what kind of a stew them dumb-headed Yanks git themselves into," Grandma said, hoisting herself out of her rocker. "Truman will give 'em what for, but your grandpa will sit there with his tongue froze up. I want you to speak up, my girl, and give 'em a message from me."

"Grandma, how can I speak up for you?" Linny said in horror.

"Nonsense," Grandma insisted. "You're a Chase, ain't you? And Chases always speak up."

Linny sighed. There was no arguing with Grandma. And so she trudged down the hill with Grandpa through ankle-deep mud, the road lighted by Grandpa's swinging lantern, and worried every step of the way.

When they rounded the corner by the general store, Linny saw in the flickering lantern light a bevy of cars extending up the hill. Everyone in town must be here, she thought dismally. The town hall was crowded, but Jared and Uncle Truman had saved two seats in the front row, where Grandpa could hear everything. Linny sat down close to Uncle Truman and clenched her hands nervously in her lap. Two rows away Cousin Joe was sitting, his small crooked body hunched up in his seat, listening attentively to Mr. Link. Jan and his mother were sitting behind Cousin Joe.

Mr. Link, the moderator, was summing up what they all knew already, that representatives of the Power Company were in town. Now he was calling for expressions of opinion on the proposed dam. "Speak up, folks. It's your right in town meeting," he said.

Old Mose Shawn, the stage driver, unwound his thick legs and got up to speak. He shouted loud enough to shake the windows: "I'm agin the Power Company comin' in here!"

Before Mose could continue, Cousin Joe piped up in a shrill cackle, "You was agin the railroad twenty-five years back, Mose, and now you drive stage for 'em."

A ripple of laughter ran around the room, and Link cautioned, "Let us not indulge in personalities but get on with the business at hand. Truman Chase, you got something you want to say?"

Uncle Truman lurched to his feet and stood heavily on his one good leg. Linny could hear his heavy breathing as he struggled to control his temper. "I'll put in my oar with Mose," he said gruffly. "And it ain't all on account of their wantin' to put my property under water neither. They want Sugar Hill Cemetery too. Folks, are we going to allow 'em to tamper with our dead?"

A low murmur swept over the crowd. From the corner of her eye Linny stole a look at Jared. He sat there quietly, without moving a muscle.

Now the Reverend Cobb was on his feet. He was a string bean of a man, with a sallow complexion and a prominent Adam's apple. The Reverend was regarded with respect by the townsfolk. His voice rose above the murmur.

"Friends, we all know that the spirit does not reside in the body that a loved one lays aside but is safe with our

Father in Heaven. Besides, I understand that the Power Company will see to moving the bodies to any site the town may choose. It seems to me we need to look ahead to what this dam will mean to our children and our children's children. We cannot always cling to the old ways. We should not fear the new."

Mr. Butterfield, the storekeeper, got to his feet. "Parson's right," he said. "Ways change. But we got to look at this practical-like. I can't say I'm agin it, but I can't say I'm for it particular neither. Do you folks stop to think that it'll take the railroad station and tracks from here to Wilmington and leave us cut off from down country?"

"We fought the railroad comin' in and now it looks like we're gonna fight it goin' out," a bitter voice complained. "And it's all a waste of breath. Common folks like us ain't got no say-so anyway."

"Who says they ain't?" Mose cried angrily.

Link pounded his gavel. "Here! Here! Look, folks, the Power Company don't aim to dictate. They want everything settled right and proper, with folks satisfied."

"Sure," the bitter voice persisted, "they want to git their way easy so's to save themselves trouble."

"Why don't you ask what the women think?" a voice shrilled from the back of the room. "What farmer ever knows how much his woman has to fetch and lug and carry? At thirty we look like old women. Power would mean help for us—hot water, electricity, washing machines, electric irons. If the women got a say-so in this, I'm for it."

"I am too!" "Me too!" Feminine voices swelled into a chorus and then broke into excited jabbering. Jan's mother had her hand up too. Linny knew that this small, dark, quiet woman was obstinate and liked to have her own way. Jan had had to struggle against her to stay in school, for in her opinion he had enough education.

Link raised his hand for attention. "Seems like the womenfolks have got their minds made up already," he said, and grinned.

"Hey, Newt, what's Calista think?" someone called.

Grandpa rose deliberately to his feet, his mouth set in a mulish line. "She's agin the Power Company," he said and sat down again.

There was no help for it; Linny couldn't let Grandma down. She stumbled to her feet, her face red as fire. "Grandma says she's a Chase and her folks fought Yorkers with Ethan Allen to save Vermont and she doesn't see any call to turn Vermont over to a parcel of businessmen that don't know the front from the hind end of a cow."

"Calista's got a good headpiece, and she's loyal to Sadawga Springs. I side with her," came a voice from the back of the room.

"Me too," said another.

Linny sat down feeling shakey, sick at her stomach, and unable to think clearly. Her hands tightened in her lap. Her head ached from the close air and the smell of warm, unwashed bodies.

Now Cousin Joe was on his feet, his old dried apple of a face screwed up in a wry grin. "Folks, we're wastin' breath," he said. "This thing's comin' sure as God made little apples, and nothin's gonna stop it, and we all know it if we stop to think on it. The Power Company can take what land they want by eminent domain."

A chorus of shouts greeted Cousin Joe's offering. "You mean we ain't got no rights over our own property?" a voice called out.

Link held up his hand again. "I was just getting to

that," he said. "The Power Company wants things settled peaceably without recourse to the courts. But they can take our land by eminent domain, the right of a government to take private property for public use by virtue of the superior dominion of the sovereign power over all lands under their jurisdiction."

When the noise died down, Cousin Joe was still on his feet. "I make the motion we empower John Link to sit in on every transaction to see justice is done. Guess we're all agreed there ain't the man born who could cheat John Link. And I suggest he have a confab with the Power Company as to how they aim to take care of the cemetery and what they got in mind as regards the transportation problem, and report back to us."

"Second the motion," Jared spoke up.

Shouts of assent filled the air. Heads nodded in agreement. "The motion is made and seconded," said Link, calling for the vote. The hall resounded with "Ayes" in answer to the motion, and Link pounded his gavel. "'Tis a vote."

There was a buzz of discussion as townsfolk thronged the aisles. Linny moved down the aisle after Grandpa, anxious to be out in the pure air. She felt a tug on her jacket, and there was Jan. The familiar sight of his friendly face unleashed the misery in her innards. Now more than ever she wanted and needed Jan's support. How could he fail to understand how she felt about the Power Company!

"Oh, Jan," she said. "It's come. A representative of the Power Company called on both Grandma and Uncle Truman this afternoon and wants to buy up their property."

"I'm sorry, Linny," he said, his black eyes serious and kind. "But lots of other folks in the village are in the same fix. There is plenty of good farmland still available. Your folks can find another farm in the village and maybe one not on top of a hill where it's a chore to do the haying."

"You don't understand," Linny broke in quickly. "The Chase place has always belonged to Chases, since before the Revolution."

"Times change, Linny, you have to accept it." He turned at the beckoning of his mother from the doorway. "I'll see you later," he said, and was gone.

Linny felt as if an abyss had opened up between her and Jan. Sadly she followed Grandpa out of the town hall. Never before in their long friendship had she and Jan disagreed as they were doing now.

When she gave Grandma an account of the town meeting she didn't mention Jan, but as near as she could remember she told Grandma every word that was said.

"So they made John Link go-between!" Grandma let out a haw. "Power Company better watch out!"

Grandpa clamped his mouth shut and wouldn't say anything.

5

THE DAY AFTER the town meeting Grandma rocked and rocked in her chair by the living-room window, turning things over in her mind. "Maybe we should get a lawyer," she said to Linny, "even if we have to sell a cow to cover the cost."

"Why don't you write to Uncle Nat?" Linny put in. "Since he's in the insurance business, he might have friends who are lawyers and would know what to do."

Grandma snorted. "It wouldn't do a speck of good. Him and Gloria will see eye to eye. They'll both be wantin' us to sell off to the Power Company and move down country to live with them."

Grandma was probably right, Linny thought dismally. They couldn't look to Uncle Nat and Aunt Gloria for help. But there must be some way out.

Grandma came up with an idea. One night after supper she said, "Seems like we ought to git Cousin Joe in on this. Likely they'll be wantin' his land too."

Grandpa unlocked his long legs from the chair rungs and reached up for the lantern hanging on the wall. "Good idea," he said. "I've been fixin' to go down to the Brick House. I hear Cousin Joe slaughtered a lamb. After salt pork all winter, fresh meat would taste mighty good."

Linny, curled up by the stove, knew what was coming

when Grandma's bright eyes snapped down at her. "Linny, you run along with your Grandpa and keep him out of mischief. Likely Cousin Joe will break out his hard cider. Hop up and git one of them apple pies on the shelf to take to Cousin Joe."

Linny eyed the line of Grandma's jaw and started for the pantry. She tucked the pie into a wicker basket.

As they swung down the back-pasture hill, the lane of firs darkened the stony path. Great red streaks in the sky flooded the purple shoulders of the hills. At the bottom of the hill Grandpa tunneled through a thicket of straggly brush. When they came up into the mowing the redness had faded and the shadows deepened. The sky was a cold slate-gray. A chill wind soughed through the firs with a lonesome cry. They tramped through the mowing out onto the road and paused for breath.

As they drew near the house, which sat in the thickening shadows where the road ended, Linny hung back behind Grandpa. Over the red brick washed by many rains hung a hushed stillness. Once there had been laughter and shouting and children scampering after the hay wagon. Now there was only this ghostly stillness.

She trudged up the yard at Grandpa's heels toward the arched white woodshed. In front of the woodpile, perched on a sawhorse, Cousin Joe was smoking his pipe. Somehow resembling an old apple tree, he sat with his shoulders crooked over and his blue-denimed legs dangling down like two sticks of wood. In front of his ears his wizened little face had a comical look. His bright eyes pranced over Linny and Grandpa, and his face screwed up in a grin.

"Evenin', folks," he chirruped, not moving from the sawhorse.

"Howdy, Joe." Grandpa sat down on the woodshed step.

"Hello, Cousin Joe." Linny crouched down on the grass at Grandpa's feet and put the pie on the ground. She was aware of the house behind her, a dark presence looming up full of shadows.

"Good growin' weather," Grandpa said, taking off his cap and running his hand lazily through his white hair.

"Yep," Joe said, not taking his pipe from his mouth.

Grandpa drew his pipe from his pocket and lit it. There was a silence while the two men smoked. Linny sat stiff and taut. She knew there would have to be just so much palaver before Grandpa would state his errand. "Grandma sent you down a pie," she said.

Joe grinned as if he had just noticed the pie. "Linny, you tell her it'll be et by tomorrow sundown," he said.

"Got your spring plantin' done?" Grandpa asked.

The last edges of the light had gone. Cousin Joe's face was blotted out by the shadows. His voice sounded like the squeak of an old cricket. "I'm a-gittin' too old to swing a hoe," he said. "I buy from that Italian who comes up from Readsboro with a truck."

"Italian, humph!" Grandpa took his pipe from his mouth and spat.

"Clean as a whistle all his garden truck is, and he's got store bread, oranges, and bananas sent up from down country. Reckon he'd stop up your way if you was a mind to have him."

"Well, I ain't a mind to," Grandpa said.

"Same hide-bound old Yank, Newt." Joe puffed serenely on his pipe.

"I heered you slaughtered a lamb, Joe. Want to sell half of it?"

"Well, say . . ." Joe hopped up from the sawhorse.

"Come right in the shed here, come right in."

In the shed Joe lit a lantern, and the wavering rays fell on the raw skinned lamb hanging from a beam. Linny peered around Grandpa's back and gave a little start. She was a farm girl and ought to be used to the sight of dead animals, she thought, ashamed of the prickles that ran up her arms.

Cousin Joe's sharp eyes didn't miss anything. "You ain't skeered of a little sight o' blood?" he said, squinting down at her.

Her eyes skidded to the big butcher knife in Joe's hand. He took down the lamb and laid it on a wooden table. He lifted the knife.

"Pshaw," Grandpa said.

Linny squeezed her eyes tightly shut, but she could still hear the muffled thump as the knife slashed through the carcass. Her eyes fluttered open. Cousin Joe was wiping his hands on an old cloth. He wrapped up the lamb in a flour bag. "Come in and set a while, Newt," he said. He creaked up the woodshed steps to the kitchen and flung the door wide.

Grandpa knocked his pipe against the doorjamb. He looked out the shed door at the faint moon climbing the sky. "Nice spring evenin'," he murmured. With slow, deliberate steps he mounted the stairs.

In the shadowy kitchen Joe put the pie on a scrubbed kitchen table. "Make yourself to home, Linny," he called back over his shoulder as he disappeared down the cellar stairs.

Linny tiptoed across the dark kitchen to the big living room, followed by Grandpa. Cousin Joe's house was bigger than Grandma's, with large square rooms, fireplaces with carved mantels, and recessed windows with wooden shutters. One little lamp set on a drop-leaf table gave forth a feeble flicker. Shadows dimmed the closed organ, and the stiff chairs had an air of waiting. She perched on a footstool in front of the cold fireplace.

It seemed ages before Cousin Joe came limping in with a foaming pitcher and three yellow hobnail glasses. He filled a glass and handed it to Grandpa, who eased himself cautiously into a wing chair and stretched out his long legs in front of him.

"I been thinkin' lately what's goin' to happen to the Brick House when I'm gone," Joe said. "You know how it was with all my folks. Us Tainters never had no warnin'—out like a light. My pa was took when he was feedin' the pigs."

"An old sinner like you, Joe, ain't ready to be took yet," Grandpa said. He took a swallow of the cider and smacked his lips. "Danged good cider, Joe."

Joe lowered his old stiff bones into a padded rocker. "Us Tainters have lived in the Brick House for generations."

Grandpa nodded. "Same as the Chases on Chase Hill," he said.

"Lately I been thinkin' of my gramp, old Deliverance Tainter. Queer, ain't it, how clear things come to mind that happened when you was a kid? But I can see my gramp standin' right here in this room lookin' like the old Nick himself, as plain as if 'twas yesterday."

Grandpa drained his glass. "Linny, you want a drop of this here nectarine?"

"Bless my buttons." Joe hopped up. "I ain't used to havin' young folks around." He handed her a glass, and she took a sip. It was sharp and stinging and warmed her stomach.

Joe filled Grandpa's glass again and sat down. He grinned. "I'll never forget the spring mornin' my gramp Deliverance come up the road singing at the top of his lungs and dripping wet. He'd got well lit up the night before down at the store, and on the way home he floundered into Lake Sadawga. He clumb on a log and lay there until dawn listenin' to the frogs. 'Those danged frogs held a jubilee over me all night,' he sez. 'On my right they called, Old Dill, Old Dill, and on my left, What's up, what's up, and then in chorus, More rum, more rum!' "

"Linny, don't you drink more than half that glass or you'll have a stomachache," Grandpa warned. "Go on, Joe. . . ."

Joe chuckled. "My aunt, Betsy Tainter, was in the kitchen churnin' butter, and Nate Chase was plaguing her to move up on Chase Hill when she looked out the window and seen Deliverance comin'. She gave Nate a shove and told him to run on home. We was all plumb scared. Deliverance didn't figger no backwoods farmin' life for his Betsy that he'd raised up to play the organ and read Latin."

Grandpa hiccuped. "Them old coots was tougher'n catamounts. Pity you couldn't a took after yer gramp, Joe."

"Deliverance staggered in the door, and first thing he laid eyes on Nate Chase. He let out a roar like a wild bull and charged. But quicker'n a cat can lick her ear Betsy pounced on him, scratching' at his face with her fingernails.

" 'Pa, stop!' she hollers at him.

"Deliverance fell back and stood there swayin' on his feet, the blood running down his cheeks, looking at Betsy stupid-like. He didn't say nothin'. He swept his hand down his cheek and stared at the blood on his fingers and then he turned and lammed out the door toward the barn."

Linny wrapped her arms tightly around her knees.

Wide-eyed, she saw the shadows in the corner quiver like a man staggering in a cloud of darkness.

And then Nate and Betsy were married, Linny thought, right here in this room before that cold fireplace, Betsy in a white dress with blue bows in the skirt. She could see Betsy's slim hand as it rested on Nate Chase's arm, and the look in her eyes.

Joe looked down into his foaming cider. "Deliverance never figgered he'd git caught short, but all us Tainters go out like a light. He never left no will. Right and the law was on Betsy's side, but she hadn't no money to fight my pa when he hogged all the property."

Betsy Chase always had it hard, like Grandma said. After she buried her young husband her hands got all rough and calloused from plowing like a man. And she struggled day and night to keep her children fed. All they had mostly was dried peas and sorghum. . . .

"There's been a lot of livin' in this old house," Grandpa said.

"Yep," Joe said. "That's why I took a ride over the mountain to Brattleboro to see a lawyer feller about the Power Company wantin' my property. Might be I could save the Brick House from being swallowed up in the reservoir."

"Kit has the same idea," Grandpa murmured.

Joe hopped up to pour Grandpa another glass. "Vermont's changin'," he said. "It ain't what it used to be, with summer folks buyin' up and mowin's gone to brush. Cows are gettin' fewer every day. Now the Power Company will finish the job by takin' all our old houses."

"Yep, Vermont's changin'," Grandpa agreed. "But you nor I can't stop it."

"That's what I think, Newt," Joe said. "I got to studyin' it over in my mind. Power Company can take the Brick House by eminent domain. I figgered it was no use to see a lawyer. Anyways, I had a good ride over the mountain and went to a movie in Brattleboro."

Joe's rockers squeaked over the old floorboards. There was a rattle at the windows and the wind sighed down the cold chimney. Linny thought with horror of the reservoir waters closing over the Brick House, like something dark and unknown waiting to pounce on you as if you were a fly . . .

She sighed heavily, and Grandpa looked in her direction.

"Pshaw, now, you got a stomachache from that cider, Linny?"

Cousin Joe flew up out of his rocker like a startled rooster. "Curse me seven ways to Sunday if I ain't got a tongue on me a yard long."

He scratched a match and lighted a large lamp with a white china base. Then came a crackle from the fireplace and the blaze of a fire. "Here, have a snow apple, Linny."

Joe was holding a pewter dish under her nose. She reached for a rosy apple. It felt real and good and smelled of the live world.

Joe lifted down an old horn phonograph from the top of the organ. "Well, say, let's have us a tune," he said. He twirled the crank and laid a round disc on the cylinder. Thin and shrill the voice leaped from the horn:

> Oh I love to travel far and near throughout
>   my native land,
> I love to sell as I go long
>   and take the cash in hand.

I love to cure all in distress that
    happens on my way
And you better believe I feel quite fine
    when folks rush up to say
I'll take another bottle of Wizard Oil,
I'll take another bottle or two. . . .

"That's the ticket, Joe." Grandpa lifted his glass. "And there ain't any better oil in Christendom than this here cider."

Joe toddled up on his old stiff legs. "For certain sure, Newt. Have another."

"Don't mind if I do, Joe. I'm drier than a covered bridge."

Joe regained his chair, rocking and rocking, his brown nut of a face screwed up in a wrinkled grin. "Don't never be afraid to fill your kettle full, Linny," Cousin Joe chanted.

"Full as this here glass of Wizard Oil," Grandpa chimed in.

Joe's rockers squeaked in time to the music, his eyes sparkled. "I'll take another bottle of Wizard Oil," he hummed, slapping his bony knees.

"I'll take another bottle or two," Grandpa sang out lustily, his old cheeks flushed pink, his eyebrows quirking up.

Joe threw a handful of pine cones on the fire, and it blazed up blue and green. Warmth danced along Linny's legs and arms. She looked with love at the two battered old faces, which had come through so many storms.

"Grandpa, you've had enough cider," Linny said firmly. "We'd better be getting on home."

When he pulled himself out of the wing chair she

thought she saw his legs wobble a little. He clutched at the back of the chair to steady himself. "Yup, your grandma will be lookin' for us," he said, and his faded eyes kindled with a gentle flame.

He pulled out his shabby leather wallet. "How much do I owe you for that lamb, Joe?"

Joe waved a skinny arm. "Take it and welcome, and come down again before summer. No knowin' where we'll be come another winter."

Linny peered up into Joe's face. It was screwed up into a smile. He cackled and pinched her cheek. "I declare, Linny, if you ain't got a look about you favors my aunt Betsy Chase."

Out in the soft night Grandpa shouldered the lamb and lurched along with his head up. The lantern swung in his hand and made rocking waves of light on the balsams. At the pasture bars Grandpa set down the lamb, leaned against the bars, and sucked in deep breaths of the cool fresh air. Linny hoped he would sober up before they got home. She wondered what Grandma would say.

Grandpa pushed his hat to the back of his head and looked up at the stars. The moon rode high in the sky. Silver cobwebs of light gleamed on balsam branches.

"Well, the earth's a-turnin', and afore you know it, snow's flyin'."

He picked up the meat and swung it over his shoulder. "Fresh lamb's goin' to taste mighty good."

He stretched down his big hand and gripped Linny's elbow. "That was danged good cider, Linny, but we won't mention it to your grandma."

His legs held him steady now, and Linny kept close at his heels in the little circle of lantern light that flashed now on pine needles, now on granite rock thrusting up sharp edges in the silver moonlight.

"Kit will be disappointed about Cousin Joe and the lawyer feller," Grandpa murmured.

Linny sniffed the rich night smells. The air was taut with the stretch and ache and urge of young things growing. She buttoned up her sweater and rubbed her chilly hands. Yes, Grandma would be disappointed about Cousin Joe's not engaging a lawyer, but she would think of something else. There wasn't the man born who could get the best of Grandma.

6.

Linny looked out the open living-room window and wished she had something to do. The air was heavy and sweet with the scent of raspberries and new-mown hay. Grandma fanned herself with a palm leaf fan as she rocked in her chair. "Where's Jan keepin' himself these days?" she asked.

"He's working at the Power Company," Linny said, thinking she hardly ever saw him anymore. When she did they both avoided the subject of the Power Company. She knew she ought to ask Jan about his new job, but she couldn't find the words. She missed the easy relationship they had always had. When she was with Jan she forgot about her skinny arms and legs and faded too-short dresses. He was always making her see things. For instance, he'd break off a flaky piece of rock and say, "Linny, do you know rocks are millions of years old?"

Jan had come a long way since the early hard days. She still remembered the long-ago day when Grandma had sent her down to the Polish newcomers with salt pork and potatoes, and she had said to Grandma in protest, "In school they call the Polacks foreigners."

Grandma had snorted. "Didn't they learn you in school about the pilgrims comin' over in the *Mayflower*?

We're all foreigners exceptin' the Indians, and we scun 'em out of their land like pirates."

Today the village had accepted the Poles. Jan could have found plenty of work all summer hiring out to farmers. He might even have helped Grandpa with the haying.

"Hotter'n Tophet," Grandma said. She got up out of her rocker and headed for the dark cellar-way. Linny watched her bend down to ladle ginger water from a crock into a quart jar. She wiped off the moist jar with her apron.

"Linny, you run out to the hayfield with some ginger water for your grandpa and Jared. Mighty hot day 'tis for an old man like your grandpa to be hayin'. Now run along. They're in the south mowin'.'"

Linny took the jar from Grandma and stepped outside into the muggy heat. The hot yellow fields were dotted with haystacks. She picked her way across the prickly stubble, clutching the ginger jar tight to her chest. She wished she could find a job, but there were no jobs in the village for teenage girls except working for summer folks, and Grandma would never let her do that.

"Here's Linny with ginger water," Jared called out when he saw her. He threw down his pitchfork. "Rest a minute, Uncle Newt." He took the jar and handed it to Grandpa, who tilted back his head and drank thirstily. He wiped his mouth on his sweaty sleeve and gave the bottle back to Jared.

Grandpa settled himself comfortably on a haystack and pulled out his pipe from his pocket. Linny and Jared sat down next to him.

"You can't guess where I'm hayin' tomorrow," came Jared's slow drawl. "Up on Pine Hill, where that New York professor bought a summer place."

Grandpa grunted. "Summer folks!"

Jared reached in his pocket for a cigarette. "What they done to that house! They have opened up the fireplaces and paneled the front room with knotted pine, and they've put in a bathroom with a chemical toilet. Now they are waiting for the power to come on so they can have electricity."

Linny listened with interest. Not a privy in the woodshed but a real bathroom!

Jared puffed on his cigarette. His eyes rested on Linny. "There's three young ones up there. One of them with red hair must be about Linny's age, I should guess."

Linny looked at Jared hopefully. Dare she ask to go up there with him tomorrow?

"A playground for the rich—that's what Vermont's comin' to," Grandpa said bitterly.

"Well . . ." Jared sprang to his feet and shouldered the pitchfork. "They bring business. They're looking for eggs. You got any eggs to sell?"

"Nope, I ain't got no eggs for summer folks," Grandpa said, and spat.

Linny's heart sank. She picked up the empty jar and looked at Grandpa sprawled on the haystack, his blue jeans faded and patched, his beard stained yellow with tobacco juice, And at Jared, sweaty in his dark shirt, burned by the sun and needing a shave.

Without a word she trudged off.

A few days later Linny and Grandpa clattered up the road toward the brook behind old Fan, headed for the creamery in Jacksonville, four miles south of Sadawga Springs. Every few days they carted their cream to the creamery, where it was made into butter that was sent down country. As they crossed a wooden bridge Linny spied three girls sitting on one side and dangling fishpoles into the water. She noted with shy excitement that the oldest one had shoulder-length auburn curls and the second one tight flaxen braids, and the smallest one had dark hair.

"Must be them professor's young'ns Jared was talking about," Grandpa said.

The girls turned around toward Linny and stared up at her with bright eyes. "Hi," they called.

Linny saw their soft leather sport shoes and colored socks, their neat shorts and jerseys, their store-bought fishing tackle, and was suddenly conscious of the straw coming through the seat of the old buggy, of Grandpa's tattered straw hat and patched overalls, and of her own bare feet and faded cotton dress. When Fan lifted up her tail and shed droppings she felt her face flush scarlet.

She stared back at the girls, but her tongue stuck to the roof of her mouth. "Hi," she finally managed weakly.

Grandpa flapped the reins over Fan's buttocks, and they rumbled across the bridge.

The next day she could hardly believe her eyes when she saw the three girls tramping boldly up Chase Hill. Shyly she opened the screen door when they knocked.

The tallest one shook out her red curls, her wide mouth laughing, and sang out, "Hello. Your name's Linny, isn't it? Your cousin, Jared Chase, told us about you when he was up haying. My name's Marilyn Brown."

Grandma, rocking in her chair by the window, thrust out her heavy chin. "Come in, young'uns," she bellowed. "Come in and let me have a look at you."

In they trooped, the small dark one looking like a doll in her pink ruffles. The one with flaxen braids swinging over her shoulders spoke up clearly. "I'm Janet; I'm thirteen. And she's Elsie. Our redhead sister Marilyn is sixteen, and all she cares about is boys. Our father is a professor in New York, and we have a summer place on Pine Hill."

Linny wished desperately she had a pair of shorts; she was painfully conscious of her old too-short dress. She saw their bright, curious eyes taking in the red-checked tablecloth, the geraniums in tin cans, the white-shaded kerosine lamp, and Grandma in her calico apron overflowing her rocker, her bushy eyebrows upspring-ing, the black hairs on her chin quivering. I hope Grandma won't slap her knee and say "Land o' Go-shen," she thought.

Grandma rocked and sniffed, her eyes bright. "Now would be a good time for all you young'uns to walk down to the Brick House and take a berry pie to Cousin Joe."

Three young faces turned toward Linny expectantly. The perspiration started up on her forehead. Cousin Joe was worse than Grandma for talking about old times. And he reeked of tobacco . . . and manure. . . .

She almost pushed the girls through the door ahead of her. Get them away from the house and then think what to do.

But they had ideas of their own. Before the afternoon was half gone they had covered the village, scrambled up the big rock in the pasture, waded in the brook, sprinted across rocky fields on tireless feet. It was fun, but Linny's legs ached and her throat felt hot and dusty. She thought guiltily of Cousin Joe's pie. She almost opened her mouth to suggest going down to the Brick House when Marilyn shrieked, "Let's go over to Lake Sadawga and see if Bill is there. He's a graduate student of Daddy's, and he's visiting us. Maybe he'll take us fishing with him." Off she streaked, up the road on dancing feet, calling for them to follow her.

The sweat rolled down Linny's face, and black spots danced before her eyes as they pounded toward the cool green lawn of the Link house across from the lake. The girls threw themselves down on the grass, and Linny leaned panting against the porch step. "Mrs. Link won't care if we rest a minute," she said.

Mrs. Link's ample figure, cool looking in crisp blue cotton, appeared in the doorway. "Land's sakes, young'uns, you look all beat. Come on up to the porch, all of you. Rest a minute and have a glass of lemonade."

It was bliss to lie on the soft cushions of the glider and look up at the glossy leaves climbing over the porch. Linny picked up a book that was lying on the wicker table. She opened it to the first chapter. *One perfect day in autumn 1677 young Hannah Coleman, who had been visiting her grandmother* . . . She read on eagerly, the shuffling of feet and the sound of giggling voices dying away.

"Who wants to read a book when it's vacation," Marilyn said in scorn, swinging the glider back and forth.

Linny swam to the surface and patted the book. "There isn't much to read at our house now, only Grandpa's almanacs."

"Linny, you take that book home with you. My grandchildren have got more books than they can read in a month of Sundays," Mrs. Link said as she set down a tray on the porch table.

Linny's dry mouth puckered thirstily as Mrs. Link spooned ice from the frosted pitcher into tall glasses.

"There's Bill. Come on, kids, quick," Marilyn called out before they could take even one little sip of the cool lemonade. Off the porch she flew on swift feet, and the others followed without a word of excuse. Linny spared a fleeting look at the tray of frosted glasses as she stumbled after them, her cheeks burning. Mrs. Link had looked offended, and she hadn't thanked her for the book either, she thought miserably.

It was a beautiful boat with an outboard motor. The young man standing beside it in bright-blue slacks and a spotless cream-colored sweater was winding a reel. Marilyn shook out her curls and unloosed her most beguiling smile. "Bill, take us fishing with you," she teased.

He brushed back his fair hair with a long slim hand that had golden silky hairs on the back. A kind of brightness stood around him. He pretended to groan. "Will you dig the worms?" he demanded, looking down at Marilyn's flushed pretty face.

Linny pushed forward. "I know where we can get worms," she said hesitantly, eyeing his clean white hands and manicured fingernails.

His cool gaze flickered over her rumpled dress, her bare scratched legs, tangled hair, and hot face.

Suddenly there was a burst of noise louder than a brass band coming down the road. No, it couldn't be! But there was nobody else who belonged to that rattle and toot. Linny's blood froze.

Bill turned. "Will you look at old 1890!" he said with a sneer.

Linny gave an agonized look. The front wheels were wobbling, the whole body shook and rattled, and there was Cousin Joe perched on the high seat behind the wheels of his old Model T, his bantam face smiling, his old straw hat on the back of his head, looking like something out of a comic movie. He had seen her. He was going to stop. She wanted to melt into the ground.

"Hi, girls," he called, snorting to a stop, his eyes twinkling merrily.

Now was her chance, Linny thought in despair. Now she ought to say, "Cousin Joe, Grandma has made a berry pie for you."

"You girls want a ride?" He threw open the rattly old door. "Climb right in," he invited. "I can push her up to twenty-five miles going downhill."

In a panic Linny saw the girls cluster around him, hopping up on the running board, laughing and squealing.

"Where'd you get the car, Grandpa? In the funny papers?" Marilyn twitted him. The girls hooted and winked slyly at each other.

But at the sound of the buzzing motor of the boat Marilyn gave a shriek and hopped down from the running board, followed by the others. Linny started after them. Above the whir of the engine she heard Bill call out, "Going to take your little country friend? Four of you kids makes a handful to manage in this boat."

Linny stopped still and waited. Marilyn was already in the boat, and Elsie and Janet sprang in after her without a backward glance. The motor hummed, and off they chugged.

"Well," Cousin Joe said mildly, "'pears as how your fine friends have given you the gate."

Without a word Linny got in the old rattletrap and sat down beside Cousin Joe.

Down the dusty road barked the jalopy. Cousin Joe leaned back and began to sing in his old cracked voice, "She'll be comin' round the mountain when she comes. . . ." Linny twisted her hands together in her lap and wished Cousin Joe would be quiet. All she wanted was to crawl away into a hole, away from everyone, away from summer folks. Grandpa was right: *summer folks!*

Cousin Joe wrinkled up his nose. "Umm, don't that new-mown hay smell good? Your grandpa finished his hayin'?"

"Yes," she said in a tight voice. "Jared helped him."

"Sure enough. Wouldn't take a cent for it, neither, I'll wager."

"No," she said, thinking painfully of Jared in his dark shirt, which wasn't clean and white like a professor's.

A long blue car flashed by, and a deep horn sounded. Leather-clad arms lifted in salute, and Cousin Joe waved back. "Hi, folks." His wrinkled old face stretched into a grin.

"Old 1890," that's what they call him behind his back, she thought, her cheeks burning.

"My egg customers," he said. "New York folks."

"Grandpa says he won't sell eggs to summer folks," Linny said bitterly.

"That so?" He burst into song again. "Sugar in the gourd and honey in the horn. . . ."

She looked in anguish at his old gnarled body lying easy against the seat back. Her throat filled. "Cousin Joe . . ." she said. "Cousin Joe . . . Grandma's made you a berry pie."

He shifted gears going uphill. "Well, now, ain't that nice. We'll have to stop and get it," he said cheerfully.

When they turned in the yard on Chase Hill he hopped out like a spry old cricket. "By gum," he said, "I almost stepped on them ants. Come here, Linny. Ants is mighty interestin' critters. Did you know they wash their faces like cats?"

There was a whole family of ants scurrying back and forth, like farmers getting in hay in the rain. Cousin Joe pulled a crumb from his pocket and dropped it. "See there," he said.

Linny leaned over to look. The crumb was four times as big as any ant, but one little fellow was tugging at it with all his might. Now his brothers and cousins were helping him tug too.

"Look how they all work together," Cousin Joe said. "Order's the name for their kingdom."

His hand swooped out and caught something from the grass. His fist opened, and Linny saw shimmering rainbow wings, long legs, and long antennae.

"Aint he pretty? Look at his velvety green coat. His ears are on his front legs. He's a musician—that's what he is. When the sun is shining he sings a day song, and when the shadows fall he sings a night song. Ka-ty-did . . ."

She stretched out a finger and touched the tiny delicate body, feeling the magical spark of life that flickered in it.

Cousin Joe's wispy eyebrows came together in a scowl. "Folks walk through life blind as bats thinkin' they're the whole show, a-pushin' and a-shovin' and a-steppin' on each other."

And run off when folks give them lemonade, Linny thought guiltily.

He let the insect go, and she watched it drift gracefully away on the air.

Cousin Joe's face grinned at her, and his eyes danced. "You just look around you and listen," he said. "All around you there's life a-bein' born and a-growin' and a-singin'. Notice how the whole shebang of critters hit it up together."

He stood still as a cat watching a bird. "That shrill drumming note you hear is a harvest fly, and that merry chirp is Mr. Cricket calling to his lady love."

He walked toward the door, his knobby knees relaxed, his bony elbows swinging out. "Your Great-

Grandmother Betsy Chase knowed every piece of grass, every herb, every flower, every insect, every weed. Seems like t'other day I come across one of Aunt Betsy's old nature books. You can come down and git it if it pleases you."

As she looked at his wizened old face, her limbs eased, and she felt the soreness going out of her. She moved close to him, not minding the homely, friendly odor of tobacco and the barnyard smells. "Thank you, Cousin Joe, I will," she said.

The barn door stood open, and she could see in a finger of light the dark bulk of Grandpa's shoulder pressed against the flank of a cow as he milked. She passed the shadowy lilac bushes and saw that a light was shining through the pantry window, and she could see Grandma's floury arms. She plucked a leaf of tansy and sniffed its tangy fragrance. Pushing open the door, she was greeted by the good smell of ham frying and biscuits baking.

She gave Cousin Joe his pie and thanked him for bringing her home. "I'll be down tomorrow to get Great-Grandmother Betsy's nature book," she said.

When Grandma heard how the girls had run off and left Linny, she gave a snort. "Well, don't you give it no mind. Mark my words, they'll be back."

And so they were. In a few days Linny heard a knock at the door. She was busily copying the pictures in Betsy's nature book with her old grade-school watercolors spread out on the red-checked tablecloth as the girls trooped in, full of apologies. They looked over her shoulder and watched while she dipped her brush in paint and spotted an oval back. "This orange one with black spots is a ladybug," she told them. "And this ugly creature holding up its front legs is a praying mantis.

Cousin Joe says some folks call them devil horses."

"Take us down to see your Cousin Joe," they pleaded.

She led them down the back pasture path to the Brick House, and Cousin Joe got out the old phonograph. When he played "The Parson and the B'ar" the girls rocked with laughter.

Day after day the girls showed up eager for activity. They helped Linny pull green shucks from the ripened corn and toss them to the cows. They gathered tomatoes hanging red and luscious on the vines and helped Grandma can them. They picked berries, and in Grandma's kitchen Linny taught the girls how to make berry pies. Days flowed into one another like golden syrup from the vat.

In August Uncle Nat and Aunt Gloria came up from Boston for a vacation. Uncle Nat, thin and tired, patted Linny on the shoulder. "I'd sure like a piece of one of your pies, Linny."

While Uncle Nat helped himself to another piece of pie, Linny showed Aunt Gloria the watercolors she had made of the insects. Aunt Gloria exclaimed in delight, "Linny, you've got real talent. I'll send you some good paints and a sketchbook when we get back to Boston."

Uncle Nat's visit was peaceful. Grandma never mentioned a word about the Power Company. Linny knew from talk in the store that the work of building the dam was going on, but no one from the Power Company came up on Chase Hill. There was no sign of the stranger. Linny felt her fears being lulled to rest, and she allowed herself to think happily of the coming festivities of Old Home Week, in which she had a part.

7.

LINNY TOOK Mart a pail of raspberries from their bushes. In Mart's kitchen she watched while Mart punched down the dough of rising bread with her usual vigor. She couldn't see any difference in Mart now there was a baby coming, but she knew Grandma worried because Mart was forty years old.

"I see the mailman's stopped, and my hands are all flour," Mart said. "Linny, run out and bring in the mail, will you?"

Linny ran to the mailbox and pulled out the *Deerfield Valley Times* and a letter. She handed the letter to Mart and tossed the newspaper on the kitchen table. Mart wiped her hands on her apron and tore open the letter.

"How'd you like a little company, Linny? This letter is from my brother Robert, who's all fussed up about his boy. I haven't seen Ronny since he was a little shaver and his ma died and I went on to New York for the funeral. He wanted to come back to the farm with me then, but his pa sent him away to boarding school."

She plunged into the middle of the letter:

> . . . to tell you the truth, Mart, I am at my wit's end what to do with the boy. He doesn't seem to have any spirit or any interest in anything. After all the advantages he's had too. . . .

"Advantages!" Mart's gentle mouth was set in a stern line. She went on:

> He's thin as a rail and getting stoop-shouldered. The only thing he cares about is fussing around with chemicals. I am hoping you can get him outdoors and help him to build up his health and take an interest in everyday life. Of course I haven't been able to spend as much time with him as I should. You know what the life of a news-paperman is. But I'm expecting to arrange things so I can take a vacation with him in the fall, although I may be called to South America.

Mart's strong brown fingers tapped on her bread-board. "If he is anything like his father, it's going to be mighty hard to keep him satisfied in the country."

"Old Home Week is coming," Linny said hopefully.

"Likely Robert won't show up. He never was one to have much imagination as to what went on in other folks' heads," Mart said, a faraway look in her eye.

"Mart," Linny begged, "let's all go to the station to meet Ronny—you and Uncle Truman and Jared and me!"

Jared drove them all to the station in his jalopy. It was a hot day, and dust flurried up from the wheels. They wiped the dust off their hot faces while they waited for the train to come in.

As soon as the train had stopped, Ronny jumped down. He was tall, and he looked splendid in his Palm Beach suit and white straw hat. His brilliant blue eyes looked through Linny and beyond, and she knew he had noticed her skinny elbows and knees, the faded, too-short dress, and her sun-darkened skin.

"Hello," he said in a chilly voice as he surrendered his

bag to Jared. His gaze flicked over the bare station, Uncle Truman's ruddy, sweating face under his old straw hat, Mart's blue faded cotton dress, and then up toward the hollow, where a handful of houses clung to the sun-drenched earth. So this, his eyes said plainly, is Sadawga Springs!

The next morning, as she was sweeping the pine boards of the living room, Grandma said, "Linny, you better take down one of them pies you baked to Mart now she's got three menfolk to cook for, and her with a young'un comin'."

The pale, arrogant face of Ronny floated up before Linny's eyes. "I was going to help Grandpa whitewash the chicken coop," she said evasively.

"Well, I guess the chickens can wait." Grandma plumped down in her rocker and waved her palm-leaf fan. "Land's sakes, it's hot. If I was a better hand with the needle, I'd run you up a thin dress. Maybe I'll get to it anyway."

Linny lowered the pie into a wicker basket and walked slowly down the hill.

In the yard the woodshed door stood open and inside she could see Ronny bent over Uncle Truman's workbench. The shavings had been brushed off, and test tubes were neatly arranged in a rack. His slim shoulders in his clean white shirt were curved over a glass tube that he kept waving back and forth over an alcohol flame.

Linny huddled in the doorway and cleared her throat.

Ronny turned around, and his brilliant eyes looked straight at her. "Get out of the light, will you. I can't see," he said.

She edged a soft step nearer the workbench.

"Look out there. Don't break my best Florence flask," he said.

"What are you making?" she asked humbly, setting down the pie basket on a pile of clean shavings.

He stopped waving the tube. When he spoke, his voice was less chilly. "Well," he said grudgingly, "this is mercuric oxide in this test tube. You watch and see what happens."

He lowered the tube into the rack and picked up a piece of wire. He fastened some steel wool to the end of the wire and held it in the flame until it was red-hot. Then he plunged it into the test tube.

"Oh!" she gasped as the steel wool burned brilliantly. She wished Jan were here to see this.

Ronny's face lit up, and he laughed aloud. "Look," he said, withdrawing the wire from the test tube. "See that reddish powder? That's iron oxide."

"Are you going to be a chemist when you get through school?" Linny asked.

He laughed indulgently. "Well . . . maybe. . . . I'll be some kind of a scientist, I guess."

"Tell me about science," she said.

He stuck out his chest a little and looked down his nose at her. "A scientist tries to find out about the world, what it's made of," he said. "He breaks things down and finds out their elements. The only thing he's interested in is facts."

She saw the light in his eyes and tried to grasp the meaning of his words.

"Everything comfortable in your life has come from some scientist's experiments—like electricity and bathtubs."

"We don't have a bathtub or electricity," she said.

He shrugged his shoulders and turned back to the bench.

"If you're a scientist, I guess your father will be pretty proud of you," she said hastily.

A tight, closed look crept over his face. She moved toward him, and her elbow joggled the test tube teetering on the edge of the workbench. Before she could catch it, away it bounced to the shed floor.

"There!" he howled. "Now you've done it. You've broken my best Florence flask!"

The kitchen door was flung open and Mart, floury arms on hips, called out, "Ronny, you screech worse than a treed bobcat."

Her eye lighted on the broken glass. "Be a good thing if all your trash got broke. Your pa sent you here to get a little outdoor life. I don't think he'd like to have you moping around in this dark shed."

Linny snatched up the pie basket from the shavings. "Grandma sent you down a pie," she said quickly, her face scarlet.

"I'm obliged to her, Linny," Mart said, wiping her hands on her apron. "Come in the kitchen."

Ronny, his hands in his pockets, was kicking sullenly at the shavings. Linny wished she were an ant and could crawl under the kitchen door. From the corner of her eye she saw his scowling face as she stumbled up the woodshed steps after Mart into the kitchen.

In the kitchen Mart took cookies out of the oven and slammed the oven door, her lips set tight. Linny mumbled a good-bye and ran.

When she told Grandma about Ronny, Grandma hooted. "You can lead a horse to water, but you can't make him drink," she said. "Maybe he'll perk up come Old Home Week."

But Ronny turned a deaf ear when everyone in the village talked of nothing but Old Home Week. Cousin

Joe got out the store-bought suit he hadn't worn in twenty years and hung it on the line to air it for his brief moment of glory when he stood up to be recognized as the oldest inhabitant.

"Good old Vermont get-together spirit," Grandma clucked as her thick fingers braided a rug for the fair. Linny trudged back and forth over dusty roads carrying a Lowestoff teapot, Sandwich glass, and Staffordshire plates to the town hall for the Early American Exhibit.

Ronny reluctantly trailed Mart's and Linny's heels while Mart rummaged through the hot attic, ducking into trunk after trunk for old stuff for the exhibit. Mart handed out heavy candlesticks to Ronny, and he scowled as he held the dusty things away from him so as not to soil his clean shirt.

"Gracious," Mart scolded, her face perspiring as she shook out a patchwork quilt, "what a lot of fuss and feathers."

"Why do you do it then?" Ronny said in his bored voice, waiting impatiently for the rest of the stuff.

Mart's face clouded. "Ronny, do you think the world began with you and is going to end with you?"

He sneezed from the dust, and a sullen look spread over his face.

"That's a log-cabin pattern, Mart, isn't it?" Linny said, quickly changing the subject.

Mart's face brightened. "Like enough, that was pieced by your great-grandmother, Betsy Chase." She held it up and looked at its soft colors. "Ronny, this country was settled by men—*men*, Vermont's chief product—though mostly we don't get the good of them the way they run off," she said with a wry smile.

She handed the quilt to Linny, and Linny folded it up and hung it over her arm, not daring to look at Ronny.

"But they never forget," Mart went on steadily. "And they always come back. It's fittin' that we should help them remember their roots."

The ringing of the phone penetrated the remoteness of the attic. Linny dashed downstairs to answer it. It was Mrs. Link, who wanted Ronny to be a Green Mountain Boy in the pageant.

Ronny excused himself politely enough to Mrs. Link, but when he had slammed down the receiver he said crossly, "What do I care what a bunch of hicks did a hundred and fifty years ago!" He looked hard at Mart, who was washing her hands at the kitchen sink. "I'm not going to get up on any stage and act like a moron." And the defiant set of his shoulders said: You can't make me.

Mart acted as though she hadn't heard. "I believe I'll make an apple upside-down cake for supper. That used to be your pa's favorite dessert when he was your age, Ronny."

While Ronny buried his nose in a book, Linny helped Mart peel apples. "I'll bet in all his travels Ronny's never seen anything like the Indian float we're fixing for the parade," she said.

Mart smiled her slow smile. "Likely not," she said dryly.

8.

THE DAY of the parade dawned hot and clear. On her way to the village Linny saw muddy Fords and shining sedans with license plates from New York, Texas, and California. Men in white flannels and women in flowered silks crowded the porches of the houses. Every house had visitors. Even Uncle Nat and Aunt Gloria had come up from Boston for the festivities.

As she climbed into the hay wagon behind Mose Shawn's black Morgans, which was waiting opposite the store, Linny's pulse beat fast with excitement. She took her place in front of an Indian tepee as daughter of old Chief Sadawga and looked eagerly for Ronny.

"Hi, Laughing Water," a voice sang out, and Jan was clambering up into the hay wagon to stand beside her. Linny looked at him happily—his sun-browned bare chest painted with blue and red circles, his long brown limbs, the gleam in his black eyes.

"Hi, Big Brave," she said smiling. It seemed like old times to have Jan by her side.

The blacks stepped high and handsome, and the Indian float bumped slowly past the store and up the hill toward the church as it followed the procession. Ronny, in his white flannels, was standing by the church steps with Mart. Linny lifted up her head and stood as straight and tall as she could beside Chief Sadawga, a giant of a man who was placed in front of the tepee with his legs spread wide apart and his arms folded across his chest, looking every inch a chief. We are history, Linny thought with a thrill, aware at the same time of Jan on the other side of her, dark, immobile, yet blooming with a kind of fertile earthiness. The summer people and Old Home Week visitors knew that Chief Sadawga had left his name to the village. They waved and cheered. But Ronny's cool eyes flicked over them with no sign of a smile.

After all, Linny thought miserably, it's just an old hay wagon carrying a skinny girl, a young Pole, and a backwards farmer with tan shoe polish on his skin.

It was no better at the baseball game in the afternoon. The Native Sons played the Homecomers, and the crowd yelped like wild Indians. Grandma pounded her cane on the floor of the buggy and hollered. Everyone was riotous with shouting and laughter and happily munched peanuts, hot dogs, and ice cream cones and drank pop out of bottles. Only Ronny sat sober and voiceless.

"Never did hear of a boy who didn't like baseball." Grandma's eyes snapped. "You ain't a mollycoddle, be you? And you a Chase!"

"Pshaw," Grandpa said, "leave him be."

When the Native Sons won the game, the crowd went wild. Even Uncle Nat and Aunt Gloria shouted their lungs out.

In the midst of the pandemonium only Ronny was quiet. Linny saw the lonely droop to his shoulders, his hands clasped stiffly around his knees, his eyes unseeing.

Mart's cheeks flamed fire red. She leaned over and Linny heard her whisper in Jared's ear, "I declare, I'm clean tuckered out with that boy."

That night, in the upstairs bedroom where she had slept since she was a child in Betsy Chase's four-poster, Linny washed up in the china bowl on the commode. As she took off the ropes of beads and the khaki Indian costume, she thought not even Ronny could skid up and down past the rows of clapping hands to the tune of "Turkey in the Straw" without a burst of laughter.

Thinking of Ronny's white flannels, she slid over her shoulders a new blue dress Grandma had made for her. In the dim light of the lamp the waist looked bunchy, and she saw that the skirt hiked up in front and down in back.

Perhaps perfume would help. She drew the stopper from a small bottle labeled "Night Time in Paris," which Uncle Nat had sent her on her fourteenth birthday. Sometimes she took out the stopper and sniffed it with delight. The only other time she had dared to use it Grandma had wrinkled up her nose and said, "Land's sakes, what's that stink around here?"

But earlier tonight Grandma had called for her cherry box. She had taken out a string of lustrous gold beads on a gold chain. "These ain't no imitation, Linny. They belonged to my ma, Betsy Chase. Her pa, Deliverance Tainter, give 'em to her when she married Nate Chase. He always thought the best was none too good for his Betsy. Mind you take good care of 'em."

Looking in the mirror now, Linny fastened the shining gold thread around her neck and hoped Ronny would notice the beads. Then she went downstairs.

Grandma pursed her lips as she eyed the dress. "I swan, I never was no hand with the needle."

Linny got a rag from in back of the woodbox and cleaned her shoes, thinking of Ronny's white buck shoes.

"Well, beauty's more'n skin deep," Grandma said,

draping her paisley shawl over her shoulders.

"That don't stop you from wearin' your bettermost best and your gold eardrops," Grandpa said dryly.

Linny wished Aunt Gloria and Uncle Nat could have stayed for the dance. Aunt Gloria would have done something about the dress.

But she forgot about the dress when they trooped into the town hall and sniffed the sweet smell of spruce and balsam. At the Old Oaken Bucket in one corner, two girls in frilly dresses were handing out lemonade to old-timers leaning on canes, their seamed faces crackling with pleasure under the soft kerosine lights that swung on chains from the ceiling. Mrs. Link in white cap and apron stood by an old spinning wheel selling chances on Grandma's rug.

Linny walked over to the stage lighted by a tin-flanked row of kerosine lamps. She looked up at the fiddlers in rusty black coats, their necks fluting up above paper collars as they tuned their fiddles. A hum of gaiety rippled through the hall. Young girls in their grandmothers' flowing skirts and long eardrops twirled on slim ankles, showing off their costumes. The wall seats overflowed with old folks and crawling babies. And there was a Homecomer Judge from New York having a friendly talk with a farmer in a scout costume. The defeated Homecomer baseball team was gathered in a corner with the winners, shouting, "Hey . . . do you remember when . . . ?"

Everyone was here, everyone, Linny thought. There was the crooked figure of Cousin Joe, and she could hear his jolly cackle as some visitor pounded him on the back and called out, "That was a great speech this morning, Joe." Spinning on her heel, Linny looked in every corner and saw them all as one, like a picture flashed on a screen, suspended in time for one golden moment. A strange little lump crept up into her throat.

"Hi, Linny," called Mr. Butterfield, scattering green dust on the floor for the dancers.

"Hi," she called back happily.

Grandma pounded her cane on the floor in time to the fiddles. With her best black ballooning around her and Betsy's brooch pinned to the lace collar, Grandma looked quite elegant. Her head wagged back and forth with the music, and the black hairs on her chin waggled too.

Mr. Link plunged to a stop in front of Grandma and stuck his hand under his suspenders. "Well, Calista, how about hopping this one with me?" Then he threw back his head and laughed.

Grandma rapped on the floor with her cane. "Git along with ye, Link. I don't notice your legs goin' any faster than mine."

Mr. Link lowered his stiff body down beside Grandma and stretched one gaunt arm over the back of her seat.

Linny had her eyes on the door. All three of the professor's children drew admiring glances as they entered, their skirts swishing, their eyes sparkling as they stood and surveyed the room. All three girls floated down into the vacant seats by Mr. Link. He turned to look at them and, sitting up straighter, said, "My, my, what have we here?"

Linny saw that Marilyn's red curls were held by shining clasps. Her green organdy dress spread around her like the petals of a flower. She bent over and brushed a speck of dust from her black patent-leather slippers.

Linny leaned across Grandma to say hello to Marilyn, and Grandma's scraggly stitches parted over one hip. She felt Marilyn's eyes on the blue dress as it sagged around her. But then Marilyn turned toward the door, her eyes alive with interest. There was Ronny coming toward them, splendid in white flannels, white shoes, and blue tie. Linny sat up straighter, covering the tear in her dress with her palm, and smiled up at him.

"Hello, Ronny. Doesn't the hall look wonderful!" she said.

His eyes skittered beyond her to Marilyn's red curls. Mr. Link got up and left, and Ronny hastened to drop into the seat beside Marilyn.

Mr. Butterfield was up on the stage. He held up his hand, and the buzz in the hall died down as he announced:

"Tonight we have a little surprise, folks. The young people have worked hard to get together a little entertainment for your benefit. The success of this here undertaking is due to Miss Eva Stacy, soon to become one of us when she marries our esteemed parson, who will now say a word."

Grandma eyed the young pastor as he decorously mounted the stage stairs. "Peeked as a Bantam rooster, no great shakes of a catch for that schoolmarm," Grandma said loudly, "though she does look like she's past her first youth."

Linny looked toward Ronny in anguish, wishing Grandma would be quiet.

The minister stretched up his skinny neck in the tight collar and swallowed. "Friends," he said, "you as Vermonters are well acquainted with the story of your great hero, Ethan Allen. You will remember how he fought for the freedom of the early settlers of Vermont, then known as the New Hampshire Grants. The land the settlers had reclaimed from wilderness in blood and sweat was claimed by Yorkers, who tried to bribe Ethan Allen to espouse their cause. 'We have might on our side and you know that might often prevails against right,' said the landlords. 'Sirs,' replied Ethan, in a historic line that has come down to the glory of Vermont, 'the gods of the valleys are not the gods of the hills.' It was the Green Mountain boys led by Ethan Allen that drove back the land-grabbing New Yorkers, who would have turned their lands into private estates."

Grandma's head nodded. "The blood that boiled up in Ethan Allen still flows, and don't you forget it, Linny. If the time ever comes when this country is in danger, it'll be backwoods folks like him that will save it."

The minister continued. "With his seven brothers and sisters Ethan was brought up in Cornwall on the Housatonic River, as yet a wild and unsettled spot. The young Ethan learned to fish, hunt, and trap, and even to travel twenty-five miles to the nearest grist mill over a blazed trail. Hardships were the common lot in those days. And so . . . folks . . . I give you Ethan Allen."

He stepped back into the wings. The curtain rolled up. Linny slid to the edge of her seat gripping the black silk over Grandma's broad knees. A little shiver slid down her back. The way Ethan Allen stood there, so enormous, so splendid in his gold-braided tricorn, epaulettes, with one hand grasping a gun, one foot thrust forward, his head up, his shoulders leading, you felt he wasn't just young Jonathan Butterfield; he was Ethan Allen himself. He was Betsy's Nathan and old Deliverance Tainter and Uncle Truman and Jared and Grandpa—familiar yet strange . . . still as death . . . yet alive forever. He was motionless, and yet energy radiated from him. He belonged to himself and he belonged to all of them—he *was* all of them, with his head lifted into free air and his eyes alight with a daring vision. She wanted to cry, and she wanted to shout.

She looked over at Ronny. He had his hands stuck in his pockets, and he was slouched down in his seat, sullenly regarding his knees.

When at last the lights came up and the fiddles twanged, Ronny still sat with that scornful expression on his face. Mr. Butterfield sprang to the platform and sang out, "Pick your partners, folks, and form in line." The fiddles squeaked:

> Turkey in the Straw,
> Turkey in the hay,
> Roll 'em up and tuck 'em up and
>   high tuckahaw
> And hit up a tune called
> Turkey in the Straw.

The lines were forming. Mart and Jared, mothers and their teenage sons, flushed young girls and bearded farmers in blue denim. Linny leaned forward and looked hopefully at Ronny. He was getting up. Her heart beat fast, and she smiled up at him.

But he wasn't bowing to her; he was bowing to Marilyn. Marilyn floated to her feet and laid her arm on his. Out on the floor, Marilyn's hand on his, the two twirled gracefully.

"It's a treat to see a smile on the face of that young mollycoddle," Grandma said, fanning herself with her palm-leaf fan.

Linny leaned close to Grandma's rustling silk as she watched Marilyn's dress swirl around her legs like petals.

Grandma's elbow pitched out. She wiped her sweating forehead with her handkerchief. "My land, child, git away. You're hotter than a little varmint."

The dancers became a confused swinging blur. One

of the lamps seemed to be rocking. Or was it her eyes? No, it was the lamp. It was teetering on its chain, pulling loose from the ceiling. It was dangling, it was falling. . . . And Ronny and Marilyn were under it! "Ronny," she squealed, "look out!"

Someone shouted, "Look out there!"

Like a flash of lightning she saw Ronny push Marilyn out of the way just as the lamp fell with a crash. Linny's heart stopped. Ronny whipped off his coat and began beating at the flames. Now he was lost in the crowd that formed around him. She saw him emerge, his hair rumpled, his clean white shirt smudged with black streaks, his clean white flannels blackened too, his coat a charred wreck.

"Guess you ain't a sissy after all, spite of them white pants," a farmer said loudly, and he laughed and clapped Ronny on the back.

"He's a Chase," someone called out.

Ronny's cheeks were flushed, his eyes bright. He even swaggered a little.

"Ho," Grandma said proudly. "Maybe he was brought up a mollycoddle, but blood will tell. Never saw a Chase yet that would turn tail."

Grandpa came up with ice-cream cones dripping from his hands. After giving one to Grandma he handed two cones to Linny. "Here, Linny, run and give Ronny an ice-cream cone," he said.

Her cheeks burned as she took the cones and moved slowly toward the circle around Ronny. The ice cream dripped down and spotted her dress. She peered through the tangle of arms and shoulders. Ronny already had a great saucerful of ice cream, and now someone was passing him a plate of chocolate cake. She edged toward the open window. She would throw the cone out on the grass.

"Hi, Linny."

She peered through the window and saw Jan outside lounging against the wall. His faded blue shirt and jeans were clean and his face was scrubbed, but his feet were bare. The fiddles started their merry sawing. "Oh, hi, diddy-di for Sals'bury Sal." His head nodded in time to the music, his black eyes dancing.

Chances were he hadn't a nickel in his pocket and probably not a good pair of pants to his name, Linny thought. His mother kept tight hold of his small wages. How could he stand there so easy and smiling with no shoes . . . with nothing . . . ?

She handed him a dripping ice-cream cone. "From Grandpa," she said.

"Gee, thanks, Linny." He looked at her. "All horsed up tonight, aren't you?" he said, licking up the last drop. "I like blue on girls. And I see you've got your gold beads on."

Linny stood up a little taller, and her cheeks flamed. Marilyn sailed by with another partner, and she caught the curious glance she gave her and Jan.

"I've got to go," she said abruptly and started back toward her seat.

Mr. Butterfield brushed by her and elbowed through the group around Ronny. She heard him call out, "Hey there, young Chase, the Jacksonville operator wants you on the phone over to the store. There's a telegram come for you."

She watched Ronny go out the door and then went back and sat down beside Grandma. There were square dances and round dances, but although she kept her eyes on the door, Ronny did not return. What had happened? Well, whatever it was, he wouldn't want *her*.

Grandma clasped both hands on top of her cane. Her

eyes were closed and her chest heaved as she gave forth a whistling snore. Grandpa had gone outside to smoke with the men. Linny got up and skidded across the slippery floor.

Outside it was cool and smelled of honeysuckle. She wound in and out of the parked cars. Then she saw a white blur on the running board of an old Ford, and her heart beat faster. She drew nearer. It was Ronny, his head bent over between his arms, his hands clenched around his knees. She heard him groan.

"Ronny," she said softly.

Silence. The only sound was the peeping of frogs and crickets in the dark.

She tried again. "Ronny."

His head lifted. He scowled as he peered through the dark. "Oh, it's you."

She hesitated as the wet grass soaked through her socks. Then she sat down beside him on the rusty running board.

"What's the matter, Ronny?"

"You wouldn't understand." He turned his face away from her, his shoulders stiff, his neck taut.

She picked a piece of tall grass and chewed on it. A car came chugging down the hill. Its headlights shone on the dew-hung grass and then flashed by. Then it was darker than before.

"They mean well," she said finally.

"Who means well?" he snapped.

"Parents."

He kicked viciously at the dirt, and it spattered up on his white shoes. "My dad never gives a damn what happens to me as long as I'm out of the way."

She sucked in her breath. "Isn't he going to take his vacation with you?" she asked, carefully casual.

"No," Ronny barked. "He's gone to South America. He's sending me to a boarding school—a military school!" His voice slid up to a shrill squeak.

"Oh, Ronny," she said in soft anguish for him.

He struggled to gain control over his voice. "I don't *want* to go to military school!" he howled.

She sat quite still on the running board in painful awareness, hearing the mountain wind cry through the trees. How old was the wind? A thousand years . . . a million? How little it cared over what small creatures it swept.

"I know," she said at last. She saw the dark shadow of his head and felt his eyes looking down at her in the darkness.

When he spoke he was less tense. "You were sent up here when you were a little kid, weren't you?"

"Yes," she said in a small voice. "Both my parents were killed in an automobile accident. I came on a train all alone in the middle of winter."

He looked up at the sky, his face naked and questioning. "Do you ever feel alone, Linny?"

She thought a moment. "I don't know. Do you?"

"My dad's a newspaperman. I suppose he'll never settle down," he said in dull despair.

She nodded her head. "I guess not."

She looked up at the black outline of the mountains. She had grown familiar with their slow changing with the hours. Now they seemed a part of her days.

"You have me," she said.

His head shot back, and he burst out in a bitter laugh. "You!" he exclaimed. His laughter stopped abruptly. "*You?*" he said in a puzzled tone.

"Yes, me. I'm a Chase. I'm your own folks." She laid a cautious hand on his arm. "Ronny, you were brave about the fire. Maybe you aren't a Vermonter, but your folks were off the same piece as Ethan Allen. Grandma said you're a Chase, and a Chase never turns tail."

"Oh . . . that was nothing." He dug his toes into the soft earth. In the shred of light she saw the lines of his face soften. He *had* liked it, the man clapping him on the back, telling him he wasn't a sissy.

"Yes, it was," she insisted. "And you look like a Chase, too. You look a lot like the picture of our great-grandfather, Nathan Chase."

He wriggled around on the running board. "Oh, him!" he said.

"You have so much, Ronny." She thought of Jan, grateful for just an ice-cream cone and a chance to listen to the fiddles. "Won't they let you study chemistry at that school where you are going?"

"I guess I can take lab work all right." He stopped kicking at the dirt and sat still and thoughtful.

"You're so smart you'll be at the head of your class."

"I usually am," he admitted grudgingly.

"Your father will send you plenty of money, and you can treat the other boys, and that will make you popular."

"Yes, I guess so." His tight shoulders relaxed.

In the cool darkness the small lanterns of the fireflies made a fitful light. She watched their instant gleam and swift-shuttered oblivion. She hesitated, groping for words, as if she were feeling her way along a narrow path on the edge of an abyss.

"And the other times . . . at night when you wake up and it's dark and you are alone. . . ." Her tongue stuck to the roof of her mouth. She lifted her eyes to the dark bulk of Freezin' Hole. "Well, you can look and look at the dark and remember you're a Chase and keep right on looking."

She caught his curious, sidelong glance. "You're a

funny kid, Linny. You look like something the cat dragged in and as if you hadn't any more sense than a rabbit."

"I guess I haven't," she said humbly.

He leaned over and planted an awkward kiss on her cheek. "Thanks, Linny."

"Oh, Ronny!" she cried out in rapture. Overhead the moon came out from behind a cloud and shone high in the sky. Through the open windows came the sound of the twanging fiddles. "Sugar in the gourd and honey in the horn." The air smelled of honeysuckle. The stars looked down.

The rest of Ronny's visit he seemed less like a stuck-up stranger. He carried in wood for Mart. He politely listened to Uncle Truman's stories about logging on Freezin' Hole. To Mart's delight, he ate liberally of her good country meals. "There," she said happily, "you'll put a little meat on your bones and color in your cheeks, and that will please your pa."

Linny introduced Ronny to Jan when Jan came up one Saturday, and thereafter Ronny spent every minute he could at the dam. He envied Jan his job at the Power Company and pestered him with dozens of questions.

"You ought to go down to the dam and see what's going on there, Linny," Ronny insisted. "It's a modern miracle."

But Linny steadfastly refused. "I wish the Power Company had never come to Sadawga Springs," she said fiercely.

In no time at all Ronny's visit was over. When he left for the military school his father had chosen, he was sorry to go. Linny saw with pleasure that he gave Mart a bear hug when she said to him, "Write to us, Ronny, and tell us how you get on at school. You are welcome to spend your vacations with us."

He answered, as if he meant it, "I will, Aunt Martha."

After shaking hands with Uncle Truman and Jared he climbed into Grandpa's buggy, and Linny hopped up after him and picked up the reins. She had offered to drive him to the station. Now he looked doubtfully at old Fan.

"Are you sure your old nag can get me to the station, Linny?"

"Of course," she answered. "We're only going to Davis Bridge. The Power Company hasn't taken down the old station yet. If you come back next summer, maybe I'll have to go down to Shelburn Falls to meet you."

She rattled the whip in the socket, and Fan spurted ahead at a good clip.

"Next spring I'll invite you down to the prom," he said. "Have your Aunt Gloria get you a prom dress. You know, you'd be a good-looking girl if you had some decent clothes."

"Oh Ronny," she sighed in rapture. "I'd love to come to the prom."

Fan shied as a car approached, tooting its horn. "Why can't Uncle Newt buy a car?" Ronny said impatiently.

"He's too old to learn new ways, and besides, he can't afford it," Linny said. Fan stopped to relieve herself, and Linny colored in embarrassment as they waited.

"Come on, get your old nag stepping or I will lose my train," Ronny said impatiently, looking at his watch.

When they clattered up to the grounds of the station the train was already in. Ronny grabbed his suitcase, mumbled good-bye, and sprinted for the train. He had barely dashed up the steps when the train started. Linny waved and waved, and Ronny waved back until the train was out of sight.

As she cranked the wheels turning the buggy around for the homeward trip, she took a long look at the station. It was a plain, square building with worn paint and a battered sign announcing Sadawga Springs. It had always been there, ever since she could remember. A lump came up into Linny's throat as she thought of it under water.

9

"SEEMS LIKE YOU need some new dresses, Linny, before you go back to high school," Mart said, sifting flour over her breadboard.

Linny leaned her elbows on the sill of the open kitchen window, feeling the warm sun on her bare arms. The wind was warm too, but it wouldn't last. Already some of the trees in the pasture were beginning to turn crimson and gold.

"Too bad I'm no better hand at sewing than Grandma," Linny laughed. "The only thing I ever sewed was a potholder I made Grandma once for Christmas."

Linny squinted at the big maple and measured it with her thumb. If she had her sketchpad with her now . . . Since Aunt Gloria sent the new paints she had been sketching trees—gnarled old apples gone wild, white birch, wild chokecherries around rotted cellar holes.

Mart stuffed the stove with wood and pushed up the kettle. "I wouldn't wonder if your Aunt Gloria would get around to see you get your chance. Maybe your Uncle Nat will send you to boarding school. A country high school is not the best preparation for college."

Linny's back stiffened, and she clutched at the windowsill. "Oh, no, Uncle Nat can't afford to send me to boarding school. The insurance business isn't doing so well with so many people laid off."

The sky darkened and the wind changed. There was a smell of frost in the air. She'd better bring in Grandma's geraniums from her windowbox tonight.

At the soft thunder of tires on the dirt road she looked up idly. There was the stage, with old Mose Shawn hunched over the wheel, his battered felt cap, which he wore summer and winter, pulled down over his eyebrows. Beside him a perky blue felt hat was turned toward the house. Linny caught a glimpse of honey-colored hair. It couldn't be . . . her skin began to prickle . . . but it *was!* She leaped to her feet and ran out into the yard shrieking at the top of her lungs, "Aunt Gloria!"

Old Mose slowed down and stopped. Light and quick as a bird, Aunt Gloria hopped out before Mose could give her a hand. "Hello, there," she sang out in her light, clear voice. "Didn't expect me, did you?"

Linny's arms closed in a tight bear hug around Aunt Gloria's blue flannel suit. Aunt Gloria always smelled of violets. My, she was like a puff of wind, Linny thought with a lump in her throat. She could almost lift Aunt Gloria in her own strong young arms.

Mart came hurrying out, wiping her hands on her apron. "For land's sakes, Gloria," she said, smiling, and she smacked her warmly on the cheek. "You come in and set a spell before you go up on the hill."

"Well . . ." Gloria hesitated. "I've got to get back to Boston in the morning. But I would like to have a word alone with Linny. You know Nat's mother, Mart. She's so decided in her opinions."

Linny picked up Aunt Gloria's black bag and tugged at her arm. Aunt Gloria pinched Linny's cheek and laughed gaily. "Wait until you hear the surprise I've got for you, Linny!"

In the house Mart said, "Come sit in the parlor, Gloria."

"Mart Chase, I'm not company yet," Gloria said. "We'll sit right here in the kitchen, and you go on with your baking."

"I was just going to make a batch of cookies and pie. Jared's out in the pasture chopping wood with a Polack boy, and his appetite's sharp at night. Linny, you get out cups and saucers, and I'll make us some tea before I get to baking."

Swiftly Mart set out plump squares of gingerbread, a mound of yellow cheese, a blueberry pie, a blue pitcher full of thick cream, and blue willow plates.

"My, this kitchen smells like home," Aunt Gloria said as she sipped hot tea and bit into a piece of blueberry pie.

"Try some of the gingerbread," Mart urged. "Are you still living in that same apartment house?"

Mart looks plain as an old milk pan beside Aunt Gloria, Linny thought, noticing Gloria's flushed cheeks and bright eyes. Under her stylish skirt, Aunt Gloria's legs were encased in silk stockings, and she had heat waves in her honey-colored hair. Linny hopped up to pour her another cup of tea.

"Yes, but I don't know for how much longer." Gloria's eyes danced. "You wait, Linny, until you hear. Mercy, child, you're all legs! Is that the best-looking dress you've got? Bring the bag here and we'll open it."

Linny's eyes widened in awe when Aunt Gloria shook out the silky folds of a soft blue print dress with velvet ribbon threading its short sleeves and square neck. "For me?" she gasped. "Can I try it on now?" she asked.

She looked shyly in the mirror at the tight waist and at the way her long shapely throat rose from the low neck.

The flared skirt covered her knees and gave a silken swish when she twirled.

"My sakes." Mart smiled. "If you aren't getting to be the young lady!"

Aunt Gloria did not smile. "You and I never had such a dress when we were sixteen, did we, Mart?" Linny wondered at the grimness in Aunt Gloria's voice.

"Well, times change," Mart said, and she got up and floured her breadboard.

Aunt Gloria drummed on the table with her fingers. "Nat's business is a little better, and I still have my job as a private secretary." There was a defiant lift to Gloria's slim neck. "Linny is going to have everything a young girl has a right to and not be made to feel like a criminal about it, either."

"There, now, Linny." Mart was stirring batter in a yellow bowl with strong, swift strokes. "Too bad you couldn't have had such a dress for Old Home Week, when Ronny was here."

"Ronny?" Gloria said, her head jerking up in a startled motion.

"You don't need to worry none, Gloria," Mart said in her comfortable voice. "That's only Robert's boy. Remember? He came to visit us for a spell this summer. With so much going on during Old Home Week, you didn't pay much attention to him." Mart turned out the dough onto her breadboard and sifted flour over the top. "Ronny's a smart young one. He's pining to be a chemist, but his pa is bent on sending him to a military school." She slapped the dough hard against the board and pounded it down with the flat of her hand.

"Some of the best people send their children to military school," Gloria said.

Linny caught the glance Mart gave Aunt Gloria, but Gloria didn't seem to notice. Mart picked up her rolling pin and began to roll out the dough with strong, sure arms. "Well, it isn't always for the best," she said.

Aunt Gloria took a piece of gingerbread. "Linny, why didn't you write and tell me you needed a new dress?"

Linny picked up Mart's cookie cutter and ran a finger around the rim. She knew times were hard in the city. She hadn't wanted to presume on Nat's generosity.

Before she could answer, there was a knock on the door. It was pushed in, and a young fresh voice called, "Could I have a drink of water, Mrs. Chase?"

Jan stepped into the kitchen, and his eyes lighted on Linny in her new dress and then on Aunt Gloria sitting at the kitchen table. He flushed to the roots of his hair and half backed toward the door.

"Step right up to the sink, Jan. The dipper's hanging on the hook there," Mart said, taking the cookie cutter out of Linny's hand.

Linny was painfully conscious of Jan's sweating bare arms and shoulders, his soiled jeans rolled halfway to his knees, his foreign-looking face—and of Aunt Gloria, so elegant and clean and sweet smelling.

"Aunt Gloria," she said, trying to appear cool and unconcerned, "this is Jan Brokowski."

Jan's face lit up. He gave Gloria a flashing smile and a courtly little nod and said softly, "It's sure a pleasure, ma'am." His eyes shone with frank admiration.

Linny saw Aunt Gloria's hard, curious stare as he went to the pump and drank deep from the dipper, the water splashing down on his jeans.

"Jan, you have a piece of pie." Mart cut a large piece and Linny watched him take it right in his hand, cram his mouth full with a huge bite, and wipe the crumbs off his mouth with the back of his hand.

Linny felt the red creep up into her cheeks. Did he have to stand there all day gobbling like a Hunky!

"Jared says you're a real good help, Jan." Mart filled her pans, whisked open the oven door, and slid in the cookies.

Linny stood stiff and still, not daring to look at Gloria.

"Well, thanks, Mrs. Chase. That pie was mighty good. I got to get back to work now," Jan said in his friendly voice and started for the door.

Never any pie at his house, Linny knew. He was hungry and thirsty, she thought in sudden shame. He had been up since sunrise, and now he'd work until after dark, and never a penny of what he earned was for himself. All week he labored at the Power Company, and then on weekends he worked at odd jobs. He was smarter than all of his classmates. He ought to be going on to college.

She followed him into the yard. "Jan," she called at his back, and he swung around. "Jan," she said breathlessly, "how are you making out?"

He thrust his hands in his pockets and drew out a fistful of silver. "We've got a roof over our heads, and the cellar's full of garden truck. No matter what Ma says, I'm going to keep back two dollars for books."

"Then you're going back to high school to graduate! Oh, Jan, that's wonderful." She glowed with pleasure. "How did you talk your ma into letting you go back to school?"

She saw the lines harden around his young mouth. "I didn't," he said. "I had to *tell* her. But I'll make it up to her. I'll do chores in the mornings before I go to school, and I'll work after school and on Saturdays." He looked down ruefully at his faded jeans. "Only thing is, I wish I had a good pair of pants."

Her heart ached for him.

"Never mind." He tweaked a strand of her hair. "My sister Julka's been teasing me to take her up on Streeter

Hill to get some butternuts before school opens. I figured about tomorrow afternoon I could go. You want to come?"

"I'll bring my sketch pad," she said, "and make a sketch of a butternut tree."

When he had gone and she stepped back into the kitchen, she burst out, "Mart, Jan's almost as tall as Jared and Jared's slim through the hips. Has Jared got a good-looking pair of pants he could spare for Jan?"

Mart was sifting flour into the bowl again. "Likely," she said. "Is he fixin' to go back to high school?"

"Linny!" Gloria said in a shocked tone. "You're not begging a pair of *pants* for a *boy?*"

"Why not?" Linny demanded. For a moment as she stood there facing Gloria, something crackled like lightning between them.

"There now." Mart pushed away her bowl. She took off her apron and brushed her floury hands. "I expect Aunt Kit will be looking for Linny. I was thinking I'd walk a piece with you around by Sugar Hill and pick a few blackberries for sauce as soon as I take these cookies out."

As they climbed Sugar Hill, Linny sniffed the fern-scented air. On every knoll blossomed the goldenrod. She slid the golden plumes through her fingers. The blackberry bushes ahead were as tall as Mart.

Linny drew closer to Gloria, put an arm around Gloria's waist, and struggled to feel the old sense of intimacy. "Aunt Gloria, I've got a new collection of sketches to show you . . . all trees."

Aunt Gloria smiled down at her forgivingly and squeezed her arm. "Why didn't I think to bring you some new paints? Never mind, there'll be plenty of time for such things. Oh, Linny, there's so much ahead for you!"

Breathing hard, they neared the top of the hill, from which they could look out over the valley. Below lay the Deerfield River winding in and out around the mountains. In the distance was the blue glitter of Lake Sadawga. Up the hill from the river slept Sugar Hill Cemetery, its thin, darkened stones leaning toward the earth.

"Gracious," Gloria said, "nothing ever changes here, does it? I remember when I was a child I used to pick blueberries in Sugar Hill Cemetery, and I suppose you did too, Linny."

Mart fanned her hot face with her old straw hat. "An old cemetery's a peaceful place."

Linny's feet skittered on the edge of a hole thickly grown over with blackberry bushes. She clutched at a prickly bush and pulled herself back.

"There's an old cellar hole over here, Mart. Did somebody live here once?"

"That cellar hole's been here as long as I can remember," Mart said. "I don't know who 'twas lived here. Your grandma might remember. Could be it was a Chase. One of Nathan Senior's brothers, maybe."

Once chimney smoke had curled on the air here, Linny thought, and a man had mowed the tall grass with his scythe, and a woman had come to the door with a cowbell to ring him in at noon. But now nothing but this hole was left—and the Power Company would fill that in with water.

Mart turned away and drifted off to the blackberry bushes. Linny could hear the soft thump of berries plumping down into the pail that hung from her belt.

A lump came up in Linny's throat. Gloria had dropped down on a piece of warm granite rock, and Linny sat down beside her and listened to the wind rustling through a cornfield below. She pulled a long piece of grass and sucked its tender end. Stretching her fingers wide apart, she felt the air flow through them. Something was passing by . . . like a bird on the wing. If you could sit quietly enough you could hear the small flutter of wings.

"Well, Linny." Aunt Gloria broke the silence. "Don't you want to hear what your surprise is?"

Linny threw away the grass. She crossed one bare tanned leg over the other and waited.

There was a mischievous twinkle in Aunt Gloria's eyes. "You deserve a chance, Linny, and you are going to have it."

A shiver of fear shot through Linny. She picked at a piece of lichen, feeling its dry, curled warmth in her hand.

Aunt Gloria waved an arm. "Of course all this was fine and healthy for you as a child. Goodness knows what we would have done with you in Boston with me working. But now . . ." She laughed happily. "Ever since the Depression started, Nat has had hard going. But things are looking up. We've got it all figured out how we can do it. How would you like to come down to Boston with us and go to a good day school that will prepare you for college?"

Linny's hands shook as she crumbled the lichen and looked off over the valley. How long ago it seemed since she had come to Sadawga Springs on the train, her ticket pinned to her coat. She had been afraid. But now . . . Sadawga Springs was home.

"It's time you had companions of your own age, dancing lessons, painting lessons, pretty clothes, parties. . . . Oh, Linny, this should be the happiest time of your life!" Gloria's face lit up.

Linny felt a sickening drop in her stomach, an icy constriction in her throat. She pulled the words up out of her as if they had bleeding roots. "Aunt Gloria, I can't!"

Gloria gave a gasp. "You mean you don't *want* to?"

Linny felt as if a pit were yawning at her feet. She thought of Jan standing up to his mother for what he thought was right and just. She swallowed hard and lifted up her chin. She *had* to make Aunt Gloria understand. Her hand curled around a tough green stalk. "Aunt Gloria, if you took up this joe-pye weed and transplanted it to the desert, it wouldn't grow, would it?"

Aunt Gloria looked mystified. Her mouth drooped in a hurt line. Her face flushed with quick anger. "It's high time I got you out of here," she snapped. "Heavens, no wonder you get funny ideas into your head, living in this godforsaken little hole with Polacks and farmhands."

Linny turned her head away and looked steadily at the shadows lengthening on the mountains. She thought with slow pain of Cousin Joe and Grandpa sitting in front of the fireplace singing, of Grandpa's lantern light shining on the firs, of Grandma telling stories about Betsy Chase on winter nights, of Mart in her kitchen and Uncle Truman reading his paper under the lamplight, of spring rains and the smell of frost and the maples' burning gold before snow . . . And of Jan. . . .

"No!" she cried out in swift passion. "I'm never going to leave Sadawga Springs—never, never, never."

Pain, despair, incredulity swept across Aunt Gloria's pale face.

In a daze of anguish Linny saw Mart swing toward them in her free, easy stride, the sun shining on her hair.

"I got almost a pailful," Mart called out. As she drew

nearer and saw the look on their faces, her smile died.

Gloria leaped to her feet and caught hold of Mart's arm. "Mart!" The words tumbled out in a rush of distress. "I've just been trying to tell Linny that now is her chance. Nat and I want her to come to Boston and go to a good day school to prepare her for college." Gloria gulped. "Mart, she refuses to go!"

Linny's eyes searched Mart's face. Mart did not look at her but off at the blue haze in the distance. "I declare," she said at last.

"Mart," Gloria said, her voice rising in a desperate wail, "you tell her what it means. Remember after Aunt Jen died how you wanted to go away to school, but Robert went and you had to stay home with your pa, and how you sat in Mrs. Link's kitchen and cried your eyes out."

Mart unhitched her pail of blackberries from her belt and slapped it back and forth against her skirt. "I haven't thought of that time for years," she said in her slow voice.

"Speak to Linny, Mart. Maybe you have more influence with her than I have." There was a bitter curl to Gloria's mouth, blue shadows under her eyes. She looked suddenly dragged out and old.

Mart looked off at the wooded hillside spotted with early flame. "Gloria," she said gently, "I reckon there's some things folks have to decide for themselves."

10

WHEN LINNY HEARD in the village that farm after farm was being bought up by the Power Company, with Mr. Link acting as intermediary, her fears grew and lay heavy on her heart. One day that stranger would come knocking again at Grandma's door.

But soon that fear was crowded down by a new worry. Mart was not herself.

First thing, as soon as Linny came in from school, there was Grandma bellowing, "How's Mart?"

Linny would make her voice cheerful. "Mart says she never felt better in her life. She's doing her fall housecleaning."

"Pshaw," Grandpa said soothingly, as he toasted his feet on the stove rim, "Mart's strong as a Morgan mare."

"That pesky Dr. Gifford don't know which way his head's turned most of the time," Grandma scolded, beating up batter for griddle cakes. "He's too old to be doctorin'."

Grandpa chuckled and sliced down a chew of tobacco with his pocket knife. "When Deliverance Tainter tipped up the bottle you said he was no middlin' man, but a country doctor what works his blamed head off travelin' night and day is jest an old fool."

Grandma's face turned a rich, ripe purple. She stoked

the fire with kindling until it roared up the chimney.

Grandpa protested mildly. "You'll have a chimney fire, Kit."

"Go soak your bonnet, Newt," she said, but she turned the damper and thrust in a chunk of green wood on top of the kindling.

Mart was all right, Linny told herself firmly. It was natural for new life to come along in the spring, with the lilacs and returning swallows—new-born calves tottering on unsteady legs, soft-eyed colts, black-nosed, bleating lambs.

But it wasn't spring—it was fall, and Mart was forty years old.

"Mart ain't no young girl to be havin' a young'un," Grandma growled. "If she had the sense she was born with she'd plan to go over to that there hospital in Bennington." She banged her bowl down on the reservoir cover.

Grandpa chewed on his tobacco. "Maybe she wants to be home, where she can see what's goin' on."

"Grandma, the Power Company can't take Mart's house, can they?" Linny begged, her eyes anxious.

"Humph!" Grandma spattered pancake batter on the gridiron with reckless abandon. "You git out the syrup, Linny," she said.

Day after day on her way home from school Linny stopped at Mart's. Mart's body grew as full and round as a ripe fruit. She walked in a lush dream, her eyes wide and starry. Linny trailed her heels filled with a strange sense of the relentless march of the days toward an appointed hour.

When frost held off and vines were still heavy with beans, Mart brought them in to can. Linny helped her snap the long yellow beans from the vines and drop them into a milk pail. Seeing the tired stoop of Mart's heavy body, Linny turned away her head to hide the childish tears. She wished Mart were younger.

"Why, Linny, honey, whatever is the matter?" Mart's warm arms closed around her. Linny buried her head in Mart's shoulder.

Mart lifted her chin and looked in Linny's eyes. She took one of Linny's hands and laid it against her dress. "Here, Linny, can you feel it?"

As Linny pressed her hand over Mart's warm flesh and felt the quiver of life, a tingle ran along her spine.

Mart reached out and snapped one of the beans from the vine. Long and yellow and perfect, the bean lay in Mart's brown hand. "I always like the time when the beans come, Linny. It's a fine thing to grow and ripen."

Kneeling among the bean vines with the sun on her hair, Mart seemed a part of the bearing earth. Mart sucked in her breath and dropped down on the earth, squashing the vines. She threw the bean in her hand into the pail. "I guess we got enough beans for today, Linny," she gasped.

Linny jumped up and snatched the pail up before Mart could hoist her heavy body to her feet.

In the house she helped Mart string the beans and cut up apples for a pie. When the pie was in the oven Mart dropped down into her rocker by the window, picked up a piece of blue flannel, and began to sew. But her hand trembled so much she had to put it down.

"Seems like a woman's life is made up of washing floors and making pies and taking care of menfolks," Mart said.

It gave Linny a turn to see Mart sit there with her hands folded in her lap, not busy over anything.

"When I was young I itched to be off to places," Mart went on. "I felt mighty bad when Ma died and Robert went away to school and I was the one to stay home and look after Pa."

Mart got up and dug out the heavy atlas from beneath a pile of newspapers in the bookcase. "See here, Linny. Here's where Robert is in South America."

Seeing Mart's flushed face and her eager finger traveling down Chile, Bolivia, and Argentina, and hearing her voice saying outlandish names seemed to turn the world topsy-turvy. Mart belonged in Sadawga Springs just like the string beans in the garden. Linny couldn't *think* of Mart's being anywhere else!

Mart closed the atlas and sighed. She sat down in her rocker again. "But I didn't feel as bad when Robert went as I did after Gloria left for the city. Gloria knew how I felt. She used to write back to me, 'Mart, get your back up and just walk out.' "

"And why didn't you, Mart?" Linny asked.

Mart picked up her sewing again. "I had to take care of Pa."

Mart looked out the window and across the brook. "Going to be a good apple crop this year. Every year, when the apples dropped down and I raked up the leaves over the iris, I used to think, There, Mart Chase, you're getting to be an old maid."

Linny crouched on the footstool close to Mart's knee. She stroked the blue flannel in Mart's hand.

Mart's lips curved into a smile. "I'd like a boy. I've been lucky with my menfolks. Not many men would have taken up with an old maid like me and come to live in Pa's house and put up with him, like Jared does."

She pressed her hand over her breast hard, her breath quickening. Her face paled beneath the tan. A look of excitement flooded her face. Then she relaxed and breathed easier. "There, I guess not yet," she said.

But her face was still pale at lunchtime. Uncle

Truman looked at her sharply, but he only said, "I smell hot apple pie."

"Hi, Linny," Jared called out as he swung through the doorway. But he didn't tweak her ear, and his eyes were on Mart's still, white face.

When they sat down at the table Uncle Truman sliced down through his salt pork and popped a piece in his mouth. "Anyway the weather's good," he said. "Summer's better than winter, and that's something to be thankful for." His eyes had a faraway look. "Never did see such a blizzard in my life."

"What blizzard, Pa?" Mart said, pushing away her plate.

Uncle Truman laid down his knife. "Guess you don't remember that far back." He grinned. "Your ma and I was living up on the mountain when I had the mill on Freezin' Hole. It was the middle of winter when you started to come, and the drifts so high I had to get down the mountain on snowshoes to fetch a doctor."

Mart looked at him, listening as if it were all new.

"I had to fight my way down through the snow," he went on. "I hated to leave your ma alone on the mountain with the wind howling and the snow flying."

Mart cut a piece of apple pie and handed it to him. "I never thought much about how it was when I was born," she said. "I suppose now is the time when you think of your own mother. It must have been lonesome up on Freezin' Hole in those days, with no car, no telephone, no neighbors."

"Your ma wasn't ever one to complain any." Uncle Truman finished the last bite of pie. "She always used to have a hankerin' for store chocolates, but we didn't git to the store often. 'Twas quite a trip on horseback." He took out his pipe and scratched a match on his overalls.

Pushing away his empty plate, he tilted back on his chair legs. "I aim to buy a woodlot over Burrington Hill way. There's a good growth of timber on it already, and in about fifteen years or so 'twill more'n take care of a fancy education for that youngster of your'n, Mart."

Jared's light eyebrows shot up, and he stared open-mouthed. Mart looked at Uncle Truman, a smile tugging at the corners of her mouth, her eyes misty. "Why, Pa," she said, smiling and pink.

Uncle Truman grinned all over his rough brown face. His chair legs came down with a bang, and he slapped his knee. "Yup, by gum, I aim to," he said.

But he scowled as he got up and reached into the glass holder for a toothpick. "Your ma was younger'n you be when you come," he said, his face suddenly stern. He limped to the door, opened it, and slammed it behind him.

Jared pulled his chair close to Mart. He laid his arm on the back of her chair. It was not Jared's way to speak out any more than it was Uncle Truman's, Linny thought, but she knew he always got up early in the mornings and made a fire in the range and put the coffee on for Mart. Now that he was doing carpentry for summer people he came back late, but he often had a bag of peppermints for Mart and a funny story to tell about the summer folks.

"Mart, I'm not going back to work this afternoon," he said, and he looked at her as if he would crawl all around the pasture on his hands and knees if she wanted him to.

Mart laid her head back against his arm and closed her eyes. But she opened them right away and sat up. "Nonsense, it may not be for days yet," she said.

Jared stretched his lean body up out of his chair. His

light brows puckered. "Mart, your pa's right. You ain't no young girl. I wish you'd think some more about going over to the Bennington Hospital."

"I guess Dr. Gifford will see me through. He's been doctoring hereabouts for forty years." Mart pulled in her lower lip and tried to keep it from trembling.

Jared leaned over and stroked one of her brown hands. "I'm not going," he said. "I'll be out in the barn tinkering. You ring the dinner bell if you want me."

Linny got up and began to clear the table. Mart let her wash the dishes alone. Linny wiped them and set them away on the pantry shelves while Mart rested in her rocker. When she got the broom and swept the kitchen floor, Mart nodded at her.

"You must be a sight of comfort to your grandma, Linny. Now you run along and have a little fun like a young girl should."

"Grandma told me to stay and help you," Linny said, noting that a little color had come into Mart's pale cheeks.

Mart picked up her sewing again. "How I loved to wade in Brown Brook when I was a young one. And to go blueberrying in the hill pasture. Once Albert Butterfield kept a bull calf there, and when I saw him I ran for the fence like Indians was after me," she said.

Mart's low laugh was comforting. Linny, pumping water for the teakettle, breathed a sigh of relief. Mart was the same as always.

"Seems like, from Nathan Chase on down, it was only the men in our family went away. Betsy Chase stayed home and plowed fields and raised her children, and she's lying there on Sugar Hill now. I dunno but what 'twas for the best I never went away. I guess I belong around here."

Linny lifted up her head in alarm. This was Mart's

kitchen, her clean scrubbed floor, her table where she made pies and cookies and biscuits, her wood range, her rocker, her white-curtained windows looking out on apple trees, maples, and mountains. A sharp pain sliced through her.

"Mart, suppose you had to go away, suppose you had to leave this house?"

A shadow darkened Mart's eyes. She began to rock gently. "We haven't seen hide nor hair of that stranger feller since the town meeting. What will happen I don't know."

Suddenly she stopped rocking and clutched the windowsill. She gave a low moan. "Get the dinner bell. Linny," she gasped. "It's on the pantry shelf. Ring it good and loud."

When Linny reached for the bell her hand shook so much that the bell slipped through her fingers and clattered to the floor. She snatched it up and ran out the shed door swinging it as hard as she could. She flew back to the kitchen, but Mart had gone from the rocker. Linny stood still in the middle of the kitchen, holding the bell, the gooseflesh starting up on her arms.

Jared burst through the doorway on the run. He cranked the phone and called Dr. Gifford. "Linny, you phone Mrs. Link," he called back over his shoulder as he bounded up the stairs.

It seemed hours to Linny before Mrs. Link came, wearing a starched white apron. She built up the fire, filled a milk pail with water, and set it on the stove.

"Linny," she said crisply, "this is no place for a young girl. You run along up the hill."

Outside Linny walked around the yard time after time and finally crouched down by the woodpile. Leaning back against the wood, she counted chips under the sawhorse. One . . . two . . . three. . . . She couldn't keep her teeth from chattering as the moans from Mart's room grew louder.

Dr. Gifford's car came rattling up the hill. He swung out stiffly and lumbered toward the house on slow, heavy feet. Linny caught the aroma of tobacco and whiskey as he drew near, and she saw the deep lines in his tired face, the purple puffs under his eyes. "Hello, Linny," he said, and patted her shoulder with a heavy hand. He went on in, and she could hear him inside washing his hands at the sink. Mrs. Link's footsteps plodded back and forth across the kitchen. Linny settled back and began to count chips again.

But it was worse when the cries stopped. She stretched her ears to hear every tiny sound. The trees, the bushes stood in a heavy silence . . . waiting. There was no sound but the ripple of Brown Brook as it slid over its stony bed. The shadows lengthened and closed down over the orchard. The sun blazed fire-red and then was gone, leaving the brook dark and a mountain chill in the air. Her legs felt stiff and cramped, and her back arched where the lumpy wood had pressed against it.

She stumbled to her feet, limped to the screen door and peered in. Jared was sitting in a kitchen chair smoking. She stepped in, closed the door softly, tiptoed over to the stove, and plucked at Mrs. Link's apron. It was rumpled up, and all the starch was gone from it. "Mrs. Link?" She looked up at her questioningly.

"Land's sakes!" Mrs. Link jumped, and a little water spilled out the nose of the teakettle in her hand. "I thought you was gone home long ago." She set the kettle down on the stove and said with a broad smile, "Well, Linny, there's another Chase. A boy."

Jared looked up, his eyes like two burning coals. He squashed out his cigarette and pulled out another. The light flared from his match, and his hand shook as he threw the burned-out match into the woodbox. "A mighty close call," he said shakily.

Linny slipped down into the kitchen chair where Mart had sat that morning peeling apples. She folded her hands together and sat quite still. The uneven sound of Uncle Truman's boots clumping across the floor seemed a long way off.

"You want something to eat, Truman? There's hot coffee and apple pie." Mrs. Link came out of the pantry with the pie and set it down on the kitchen table. This morning Mart had peeled the apples and baked that pie, Linny thought.

Uncle Truman looked down at the pie. "No, I don't want nothin' to eat." He grinned from ear to ear. "I'm goin' out to buy a woodlot for my grandson." The door slammed, and he was gone.

Dr. Gifford came in and swung his worn bag up on the table. Mrs. Link poured hot water from the teakettle into the washbasin in the sink. He scrubbed his hands noisily and threw the soap back into the soap dish. He looked at Jared. "You can stop worrying, Jared," he said. "Mart isn't any young girl, but I believe she'll be all right now. But, Linny, you better wait until tomorrow before you go in to see her. Let her sleep."

He dried his hands on the kitchen towel. His face looked old and tired but relieved.

Mrs. Link poured him a cup of steaming coffee and cut a piece of pie. "I suppose you got a good way to go yet," she said. "Better have a bite."

He drew up a chair and stretched his legs under the table. He cut off a bite of the pie and gulped it down. "Good pie," he said.

Jared disappeared into Mart's room. It was getting dark. Mrs. Link lighted the lamp and set it in the middle of the kitchen table. Dr. Gifford finished his pie, picked up his bag, gave them a weary good-bye, and was gone.

Mrs. Link climbed the stairs to Mart's room and came back with a wicker basket, which she set up on two chairs. "Got a Chase look about him all right, Linny, and a sight of red hair," Mrs. Link said.

Linny excitedly got up and looked into the basket. She felt as in a daze.

The baby's eyes were closed and his fists doubled up, and he gave a thin little cry like the squeak of a kitten. Then suddenly his eyes opened and he looked straight at her.

"Hello, little cousin," she said huskily. She stretched out a forefinger, and a flower-petal fist closed tightly around it.

Mrs. Link leaned over and pulled up the blanket a little. "Funny thing how women act. I've known Mart all her life, and she was a bright girl at school. She'd have given her eyeteeth when she was a young one to get away from Sadawaga Springs. Many a time she's cried her eyes out in my kitchen. But when her time come, she says to Jared, 'Call him Nathan Chase.' Mrs. Link wiped her eyes with a corner of her apron. "Birth or death's a common thing, common as grass. We keep on goin', and we keep on comin', and 'tis mighty hard to make head or tail of it."

She straightened up and moved around the kitchen pouring water into the dishpan and washing dishes with a clatter.

Like a sound penetrating a dream, Linny suddenly became aware of someone pounding on the kitchen door. She threw it open, and there stood the stranger from the Power Company. In the near dusk he was outlined against the dark mountains by his white linen suit and white straw hat. There was a pleasant smile on his rosy face.

"Good evening," he said, his voice smooth as cream. "Is Mr. Truman Chase or Mrs. Jared Chase at home?"

Linny's hands clenched, the nails biting into her palms. The face under the white hat blurred, became a dull ghost dissolving into the shadows. With an effort she tore out the words. "Mr. Chase is not home, and Mrs. Chase is not seeing anybody today."

She wondered with a choking fury if his next stop would be on Chase Hill.

11

THE HAYSTACKS were gone from the fields, and the summer folks had returned to the city. The wind blew, rising and falling like sea waves, beating against gray clapboards and loosening barn hinges. The maples blazed scarlet and gold before dropping their leaves, and the air was tangy as spiced cider. The hills turned dark purple, and early mornings found the grass tops whitened and hollow cornstalks turned black. The churning brook leaped over its stony bed. Silence shrouded the meadow, broken only by the brittle snap of bare branches creaking with cold.

"Days are gittin' shorter," Grandpa sighed, and took the lantern with him when he did his chores.

Linny treasured every hour. "Potato time is best," she said to Jan when he came to help her finish digging the potatoes. The paling sun was like gold in her veins, and the wind smelled of fall. The fields yielded up corn, pumpkins, winter squash, and onions. She would throw down the potato digger, rip off her cotton work gloves, and plunge her bare hands into the earth, bringing up a potato. Shaking off the dirt, she felt it in her hand solid and perfect.

With Jan's help all was snug in the Chase house. Ears

of corn hung from the attic rafters. Potatoes and apples filled barrels in the cellar. The pigs were butchered, and Grandma tried out the fat for lard. On the pantry shelves gleamed jar after jar of jelly: wild grape, plum, the pale gold of crab apple, the deep wine of wild chokecherry. Tall glass jars of peas, string beans, carrots, and relish gave promise of plenty against the winter.

Back at school, wearing the blue dress Aunt Gloria had brought her, Linny found the work easy with the exception of mathematics. She planned to get Jan to help her with that. He would find time in his busy life.

Each morning she met Jan at the general store. Jan looked presentable in the blue gabardine trousers Jared had given him and a new shirt his mother had let him buy. At the store they climbed into the shabby school bus driven by old Mose Shawn. In rain, hail, or snow old Mose transported the village teenagers to the dingy old high school on Jacksonville Road. For years there had been talk of a new schoolhouse, but when it came time to vote funds in the town meeting, the decision was always in the negative.

"Someday, when the town gets the Power Company taxes, there will be a new schoolhouse, but you or I won't get the benefit," Jan said.

"I've always loved the old schoolhouse. It seems like home," Linny said, wishing that time could stop right now and not go any farther. Next June she would have to find some way to earn a living or go to college, as Uncle Nat and Aunt Gloria wanted her to. Jan was the one made for college, she thought.

"Jan, I wish you would think some more about going to college. I know you could get a scholarship," she said.

"There you go again, trying to get me away from the

Power Company," Jan said with a twinkle in his eye. "It won't work. I have a good start there now, and next summer they'll push me ahead. You'll see. Someday I'll be a superintendent. You just have to get used to the Power Company, Linny. It's a fact of life. Work on the dam has already begun, and someday the dam will be finished."

Linny knew work was going on at the dam, because before snow fell a tide of workers swept through the village. Men with mighty muscles and wind-bitten faces, men with husky shoulders and brawny chests, men lean and bandy-legged, men small-boned and swarthy, or tall and blond, men with thick accents—Poles, Hungarians, Swedes, Italians, Irish—every race, creed, and color swarmed into swift-born rooming houses and into every spare bedroom in the village. Rough board houses sprouting tin stove-pipe chimneys mushroomed up along the banks of Sadawga Lake. Even boxcars drawn up on sidings were used to live in. North of the dam site a small town shot up, erected by the Power Company to feed and house the endless flow of workers. With their coming the face of Sadawga Springs had changed overnight.

Linny and Grandpa, riding behind Fan over the leaf-strewn roads to the Jacksonville creamery, stared at the bleak shacks where sometimes they caught a glimpse of a swarthy face or a dark-eyed child. Once a person could look across the road from a neat white farmhouse to a lush meadow sloping to the water's edge of the lake. Now the view was cut off by the huddled shacks squatting close together in dismal sameness. A long wind rose and swelled, rattling the matchstick stove-pipes from which thin wisps of smoke threaded the gray of the sky.

"Come winter, a good blow'll carry them flimsy things

to Jerusalem," Grandpa said, slapping the reins on Fan's slow-moving rump.

Linny shivered. No cellar to store apples, potatoes, and pork against the winter. No attic to hang up corn or herbs for winter sickness.

A swarm of half-clothed, dirty children was playing in the leaves with some old tin cans.

Grandpa's blue eyes darkened to match the sky. "Driftin' foreigners," he muttered through his beard. "Bring up their young'uns like hogs."

As soon as Linny and Grandpa set foot in the house, Grandma demanded, "Why don't nobody ever tell me what's goin' on in this town?"

Linny's lips tightened. "The wind's getting chilly, Grandma, and it smells like snow," she said.

But of course there was the telephone. When Grandma, listening in, heard that old Dr. Gifford had retired and that the old parsonage across from the store had been turned into a small hospital staffed by a young couple from the city, Dr. and Mrs. James Adams, she clucked and said, "There, that's what this town has been needin' for years."

"Catnip tea was always good enough for me," Grandpa said, going right on shucking corn for the hens.

"And I heard there was cars from Florida and Texas parked up in the Wheeler yard." Grandma's bright eyes snapped. "Land's sakes, I ain't never been outside Windham County in my life."

"Pshaw," Grandpa said, "where's there to go to?"

Linny waited in a sweat for Grandma to hear about the springhouse. The rusty, creaking pump from which had gushed ice cold, pure "iron water" had been carted away and the rustic lattice springhouse torn down. "Why, that springhouse had stood there for near a century," folks muttered darkly. When a new log cabin sprang up on the spot with a long bar inside, where bottles clinked and men shouted and sang on cold winter evenings, townsfolk hearing the rumpus closed their blinds and sniffed, "Scum. Riffraff."

The evening goings-on at the log cabin were discussed daily at the store. Linny heard Grandpa say to the knot of men trying to warm their hands over the stove, "What can you expect of foreigners!"

"Still the same old hide-bound Yank, ain't ye, Newt?" Cousin Joe cackled. "Guess you forgot Vermont was cleared on Jamaica rum, and time was when the parson used to announce from the pulpit when a new barrel of rum come to town."

"Sure thing," Mr. Butterfield said. "Why, I remember my pa tellin' how in the old days they used to give cash customers of the store a drink of rum when they come to buy." He ran a gaunt finger over his chin. "I call to mind a story he used to tell on your pa, Joe. Caleb Tainter never parted with a penny; he always traded."

"Yep," Joe squealed. "I remember he used to walk three miles to read the free newspaper at the store and save two cents."

"Well," Mr. Butterfield went on, his long face serious, as if he were commiserating with a mourner, "this day he come in and put down a penny and sez, 'Now give me a drink of rum.' And when my Pa drawed off the rum he sez, 'Now break an egg in it!' "

Loud guffaws circled the stove. Cousin Joe shook with laughter.

"Sure they drunk rum," old Mose Shawn wheezed. "Them was hard days with hard work to do."

"Well," Joe drawled, "I wuz down to the dam and seen 'em handle them derricks and trucks, and the vibrations enough to shake your guts to pieces. And there ain't a smidgen of heat in them little cabooses, and they handle them levers bare-handed. Crimus, I dunno how they ain't froze to death. If I was one of them, come night I'd warm my vitals with lye if nothin' else was handy."

Grandpa turned a deaf ear. He stowed away salt and tobacco in his big pockets. "Guess it's time we was shovin' on home, Linny."

When Grandma found out about the springhouse she turned on Grandpa in a fury. "I want to know!" she thundered. "Don't you go keepin' things from me. I want to know what's goin' on in this town!"

Neither Grandpa nor Linny would go near the dam. They left it to the Reverend Cobb to report the dam's progress to Grandma. The whole village knew that every chance he got, the Reverend stole down to the dam to stand transfixed at the giant derricks scooping up the earth.

"Why, those derricks hold half a ton of dirt," he said to Grandma, his thin face alight, his Adam's apple moving up and down in excitement. "Visitors from all over New England are coming to see the stream of water hurling from the hydraulic pumps flinging water twenty feet in the air. A sight, I tell you."

"How high's the dam going to be?" Grandma demanded.

"Two hundred feet, the highest earth dam in this country. The reservoir will stretch back twelve miles to Wilmington, covering twenty-three hundred acres. Counting the power house, diversion tunnel, pressure tunnel, spillway, and transmission lines, the cost will run upwards of eighteen million dollars."

"Have some spruce gum," Grandma clucked, offering the Reverend a crumbly handful. He accepted a piece and chewed vigorously.

"The tunnel is being built by blacks from Kimberly,"

he went on. "Think of that, from the African diamond mines. Handsome creatures they are too, and God's children same as us."

"How they aim to git through the mountain?" Grandma's bushy eyebrows pulled together.

"They're blasting," the parson said, his face rapt, "blasting through the mountains, right through rock for two and a half miles. A wondrous age! An age of miracles!"

"Humph," Grandma grunted, her rockers pounding the floorboards. "I'd give a dollar to see them explosives set off."

But the news from the dam was not always so exciting. Sometimes it was bone chilling as on the day when Grandpa brought home news that the first man who went into the tunnel at the dam had not come out under his own power.

It got to be an old story. Time after time Linny stood beside Grandpa and watched while a fresh grave was dug in the new cemetery, feeling her skin prickle as it used to when she was a child and saw Grandpa hold a hen's neck on the chopping block and pick up his ax.

"Well," Grandpa admitted grudgingly, "they were foreigners, but they died with their boots on."

Death was no stranger to Sadawga Springs, Linny knew. But these men had not lived out their allotted three score and ten. They were neither brittle-boned nor white-headed. They had swung along the road, their plaid shirts half open, exposing hairy chests. When the dirt closed over them there was no eye to weep, no tongue to remember whether they were partial to mince pie or apple dowdy. If there was a woman, she melted silently out of town. Another man filled the gap, and the work went on.

"Makes out a human being ain't no more account than an ant," Grandpa said.

One day on the school bus Linny told Jan she had seen an Italian being carried on a stretcher into one of the board shacks and heard the loud wailing of the women and children.

Jan said patiently, "It's too bad, of course, but it has to be. Every dam that's built costs a few lives. Linny, you take a look at the gravestones in any old Vermont cemetery, and you'll find whole families wiped out within a few days. Why, ten to one, more lives were lost here in the village from one typhoid epidemic than in the building of three dams."

But Linny's eyes were stormy, her mouth set in the stubborn Chase line. After school she slipped off into the chilly pasture by herself and sat down on a ledge beside a scrub apple tree, her sketch pad in her lap. Now that the leaves were gone it was a good time to sketch the bare shapes of trees.

But instead of trees she found her pencil crudely outlining the square face of a Swede, or a small-boned Italian buying snuff in the store, or a brawny Irishman. The habit grew on her of staring up from under her lids at the wind-hewn faces she met in the road and trying to learn the curves by heart. She hid the sketches under the feather tick on her bed and never showed them to anyone.

Although the workers were strangers to her, she never became reconciled to their violent deaths. Her stomach fluttered as always the night Grandpa brought home the news from the store that they had had to carry Sven Peterson out of the tunnel. She thought of old Mose Shawn, who had struck up a friendship with Sven. The next morning in the school bus Linny and Jan looked at the stiff back of old Mose, not knowing what to say.

"Too bad about that Swede who was caught in the explosion yesterday," Jan ventured.

Old Mose took off his felt cap, which was as much a part of him as his nose, and settled it back on his head. "Yep. We used to swap jokes. He could tell a dang good story even if he was a Hunky."

"I hate the dam!" Linny burst out. "I hate it! I hate it!"

"You ought not to feel that way, Linny," Jan said, his voice patient and understanding. "When the pioneers cleared this land they had to fight Indians, and some of them got scalped. Now men take their chances with machinery. There's always risk."

"At least an Indian was a human being, and you could fight back," Linny cried passionately.

The dam seemed to intrude itself into Linny's life in more ways than one. When old Mose Shawn and his shabby bus gave way to a new school bus driven by a French Canadian, Linny felt as if the ancient maple in front of the house had been struck down by lightning. She missed old Mose, missed his leisurely ways and his vivid stories. She couldn't get used to Hopping Frog, as the townsfolk called the Frenchie. He was always in such a hurry, dark and silent and driving like a madman. Now she had to start early to get down the hill to the store, because he left on the dot.

One morning, late and hurrying, she slipped on a patch of dead leaves by the log cabin. Her feet shot out from under her, and her books and school papers scattered to the wind. Wiry old arms yanked her to her feet, and she looked up into Mr. Butterfield's long gaunt face.

"Goin' to a fire?" he said mildly.

She looked beyond him to the store, where a man on a ladder was painting the weathered boards a dazzling white with turkey-red trim.

"Why, Mr. Butterfield," she gasped, "you're having your store painted."

He shook his head. "Nope," he said, "I ain't."

She brushed smudges of dirt off the back of her coat and waited for his manner of telling it.

"It ain't my store no more." He crooked a knotted finger over the bridge of his nose and stared down at her, his eyes like the eyes of a sad old horse.

A queer drumming was in her ears as she bent down and picked up her Latin book and her history book, which were both lying face down in the road.

"There's been a Butterfield in that store for four generations." He sighed and laid a hand on the small of his back. "But my son Jonathan never took to it. He's gone to Boston to work in a machine shop. Without his help it was gettin' much too much for me with all that trade from the Power Company folks. I sold out to one of these here chain concerns that's been plaguing me for the last six months."

The school bus was coming, but Linny hesitated, seeing the stoop of Mr. Butterfield's gaunt frame.

"Good-bye, Mr. Butterfield," she called back over her shoulder and flew toward the store. The driver wouldn't wait for her, not like old Mose Shawn.

Every day as she went back and forth to school Linny caught glimpses of painting going on inside the store and of glass cases being set up.

On Friday night as they stepped down from the bus Jan caught her arm. "Come on, Linny, let's go in and see the new store."

The door closed silently behind them as they stepped

in, and Linny stood still until she realized she was waiting for the familiar tinkle that used to summon Mr. Butterfield from the depths of the back room. The pickle barrel that had always stood by the door was gone. So was the barrel of crackers. "Not giving anything away, are they?" Jan said with a grin.

The potbellied stove, around whose warmth men had sat in tilted-back chairs discussing the President and the weather, had been replaced by a smug oil burner. On its smooth surface there wasn't any place to put your feet, and not a chair was in sight. The old spittoon had vanished too, along with the mingled odors of molasses, spices, kerosine, and tobacco juice. A faint aroma of disinfectant hung in the air.

Jan stared in awe at the newly painted shelves where, in even rows, a miraculous assortment of canned goods, soaps, and breakfast foods stood, their prices clearly marked.

"Look over here," he said to Linny, and they stepped across the clean floor to the glass cases. They looked down at red meats lying in white enamel trays. "Better than salt pork," he said.

Linny's eyes grew dreamy. "I remember in the spring, after salt pork all winter, it was a great occasion when Cousin Joe slaughtered a lamb. Then Grandpa and I used to go down the back-pasture lane to the Brick House to buy some of the meat from him."

Jan nudged her in the ribs. "There's your grandpa now," he said, "just coming in."

"Grandpa," Linny called out, and beckoned to him. "Look here, they've got fresh meat."

Grandpa's eyes went around the room, not missing a trick. With his slow, deliberate step he moved up to the counter and laid down two paper parcels. His eyes twinkled as he eyed the black-lettered name plate on the wall that said "Harold Eames" and then the spruce, clean-shaven young man in a white apron who said briskly, "Can I help you, sir?"

Grandpa shoved his bundles across the counter. "Here you are," he said. "Two pounds of fresh-churned butter and two dozen new-laid eggs. I'll trade for a bag of salt and some of that there fresh beef."

The young man pushed the bundles back across the counter. "I'm sorry, sir," he said politely, a bright smile on his face. "This concern doesn't do trading anymore. We only do business here on a cash basis."

The door burst open, and the men from the dam flooded in, their steaming bodies and raucous voices filling the store. Coins rattled on the counter. "Come on, young dandy, step lively," they shouted. "We ain't got all day."

Jan picked up the eggs and butter and walked to the door with them, his firm hand under Grandpa's elbow. Outside he handed the parcels silently to Linny.

Jan knew as well as she did what this would mean, Linny thought. Grandpa's small outlay of cash went for taxes, what tools he needed, and clothes.

"Thanks, Jan," she said, and she and Grandpa turned up the hill.

The cellar was full of potatoes and apples. The pantry held rows of vegetables grandma had put up from the garden. But how would they get along without flour and salt and sugar and tea and kerosine? And for the winter they would need new boots.

"Maybe the folks who work down at the dam will buy Grandma's butter and eggs," she said, swallowing hard.

Grandpa made no answer. His head was sunk down on his chest as they trudged up the hill.

I'll have to write and tell Uncle Nat, she thought, her heart sinking. And Grandpa will hate that.

As they passed the log cabin the door stood open. The long bar was crowded, and the glasses clinked merrily.

12

TAXES WERE DUE in November, and the day of reckoning drew steadily nearer. Linny knew that in spite of hoarded savings, the brown earthen teapot on the pantry shelf was far short of enough cash to pay the taxes. Soon snow would be flying, she thought with a sinking heart, and she sat down to write to Uncle Nat that the taxes were due.

The north wind stripped the leaves and sounded its winter warning. Linny thought how Aunt Gloria would complain about the cold. She went through the chilly parlor into the bedroom beyond to make up the bed. She might heat a brick in the oven and wrap it in flannel, as Grandma used to do for her when she was a child. The brick would warm the icy sheets. And a fire in the parlor stove would help to warm the guestroom.

With a new blast of cold, Uncle Nat and Aunt Gloria came, carefully cheerful, a look of determination on their faces. But they went to bed that night without a word.

The next morning Linny awakened to a clatter in the Franklin stove in the parlor below. Grandpa's trying to warm the house up for Aunt Gloria, she thought, and hopped out of bed, her teeth chattering as she pulled on warm underwear, a woollen skirt, and a sweater. Downstairs she ran quickly out into the woodshed, leaving the door wide open as she loaded up with wood. When she burst back into the kitchen, she found Aunt Gloria in a thin silk negligee brushing her teeth at the kitchen sink.

"For goodness' sake, Linny, shut the door. That draft is enough to chill a corpse," Gloria complained.

Linny dumped the wood in the woodbox and sprang to shut the door.

Grandma, warming the iron griddle on the stove, let out a haw. "Gloria, if you was to git a little meat on them bones, you wouldn't mind a breath of fresh air."

"Anybody who weighed two hundred would find that privy in the woodshed as cold as Greenland," Gloria grumbled.

Uncle Nat blew in rubbing his fingers, his narrow shoulders hunched toward his chin. "I need a corkscrew to loosen up my bones," he muttered, holding his hands over the stove. "Come winter, this old house isn't fit to live in."

Gloria shivered as she wrapped her negligee closer around her. "You're right, Nat," she said. "The wind sweeps in under every door and window in the place."

"Some good hot coffee will warm you folks up, and Grandma's got the griddle cakes all ready," Linny said, trying to sound bright and cheerful.

Gloria dressed quickly, and Linny lent her a warm sweater. She waited anxiously to see what they would say. But it was not until they had devoured a golden stack of pancakes, crisp bacon, doughnuts, and coffee laced with thick cream that Uncle Nat, replete as a stuffed goose, pushed back his chair from the table and began.

"Now, Pa, don't go and get up on your high horse. Let's talk things over sensibly. Gloria and I have got a proposition to make."

116

"That's right," Gloria chimed in. "Give Nat a chance to explain before you jump all over him."

Nat squared his shoulders and drew a deep breath. "The thing is, Pa, the game is up. I've seen this coming for a long time."

Linny's eyes widened. She couldn't sit still. She got up and began clearing away the dishes.

Nat leaned forward, his voice patient as if he were speaking to a not-too-bright child. "Pa, you can't hope to compete with these big Western farms that specialize in one crop. Farming is a business, and they run it like any other business, with an eye to the profits."

Grandpa teetered back on his chair legs and regarded his toothpick holder thoughtfully. "Wal, I ain't never made a profit of ten thousand dollars in a season, like some of these here Western fellers. But when they fall, they fall harder. They got further to go. We ain't never gone hungry yet, nor in debt neither. And our soil is nailed down. It ain't like out in Oklahoma and Kansas, where dust storms blew farmland clear to the ocean."

Grandma sniffed. "Vermont is weatherin' the Depression better than any state in the Union."

Gloria shook her head. "That's because Vermonters can turn their hands to any trade. Pa, look how Jared gets along. He's a good carpenter, always in demand by summer folks. There's fern picking, cutting Christmas trees, making maple syrup, working on the roads. All the farmers around here turn to any kind of odd jobs to piece out their cash."

"Gloria's right," said Nat. "But, Pa, you can't work like that anymore. And the time's gone by when you can scratch a living out of a rocky little hill farm."

Grandpa puffed calmly on his pipe. "What you got in mind, Nat?"

Uncle Nat's chest expanded. "Gloria and I want to do

117

our part. I've got my eye on a nice modern house in a suburban development, big enough for all of us. We'll sell out here to the Power Company, and you folks can come live with us." He beamed as if he were conferring life's greatest blessing on them.

Grandpa tugged at his beard. "I dunno's I'd know how to git along in a city."

Linny saw it coming, saw Grandma's bushy eyebrows pull together, the black hairs tip up on her chin, heard the sharp intake of her gusty breath. She handed Grandma her cane, and Grandma got to her feet.

"I was born on the Nate Chase place, and I aim to die on it," she exploded.

Gloria shrugged her shoulders. "There, Nat, what did I tell you? I knew that's the way it would be. They're too stubborn."

Uncle Nat's face turned livid. "I can't keep up two establishments in this Depression, and nobody with any sense would expect it," he said.

"Ain't nobody askin' ye to," Grandpa said.

"Snow will be on you before you know it. How do you think you are going to meet the taxes?" Uncle Nat demanded.

Linny held her breath, a chill in the pit of her stomach.

Grandpa struggled to his feet and settled his moth-eaten felt hat on the back of his head. He reached for the milk pail and slung it over his arm. "I ain't just thought yet, but it'll come to me," he said with calm dignity.

Later, when Uncle Nat and Aunt Gloria were packing up to go back to Boston, Linny overheard Uncle Nat say, "We can't get soft-hearted and give in. If we stick to our guns they'll have to come around."

Gloria agreed. All the same, before she left she tucked

a crisp bill into Linny's hand. "I wish you'd be sensible and try to see things our way, Linny. They are too old to go on living here, and you are too young to run the farm."

Linny felt a choking in her throat as she looked at Gloria's wistful face. She felt as if she were trying to shout across the wind. "Don't worry about us, Aunt Gloria," she said gently. "We'll be all right."

But things were far from all right, Linny knew. It was hard to concentrate on her school lessons. She made up her mind to talk things over with Mart and tell her about Uncle Nat's proposal for them to move to the city. What a comfort it would be to see Mart's calm face and share with Mart her nagging troubles.

But when she pushed open the kitchen door of Mart's house, she saw at once that something had happened to Mart. She was in the kitchen rocking the baby, and there were tears in her eyes.

"Come in and sit a minute, Linny. I've got something to tell you," she said.

Linny sank down on a stool, her thoughts churning. If Mart was crying, it must be bad news. "You haven't lost your house to the Power Company?" she gasped.

Mart nodded her head. "It's come. Pa had to sell out."

Tears stung Linny's eyelids. "What are you going to do, Mart?" It was impossible to think of Mart's house under water.

Mart rocked vigorously. "It's all decided, but I'm not sure it's for the best. Jared and I thought we'd get a place of our own, but Jared's mother, Sophronie Chase, insists we come to live with her in Jacksonville. She's got that big ark of a house and is all alone." Mart sighed. "Pa don't like it a bit. Seems as if there's always old folks to look after. How's Aunt Calista? She'll take it hard when she hears about Pa."

Linny nodded. "I'll tell her, Mart," she promised. Mart had enough on her mind without being burdened with their troubles, Linny thought, and went away without saying a word about the taxes coming due.

When she told Grandma about Uncle Truman's house being sold to the Power Company, Grandma burst out, "I vum, it ain't like Truman to give up so easy. He should have waited until we got a Bennington lawyer on the job."

As Linny went back and forth to school, it seemed strange to see Mart's house deserted. There was no sign of life around the place, although Uncle Truman still hadn't moved out. He refused to go to Sophronie Chase's house and he kept to himself.

When Mart telephoned from Jacksonville and asked Linny to come over, Linny had a sudden inspiration. Maybe she could talk to Jared, and he would have some idea of how they could get out of the fix they were in.

A few days later Linny harnessed Fan to the buggy. "You rest yourself, Grandpa. I'll take the cream over to Jacksonville," she said. No need to mention she planned to see Jared.

At the Sadawga Springs post office she jumped down and went in for the mail. Sometimes there was a card or a letter from Ronny. His father had followed Mart's advice and not sent him to military school after all.

Linny twirled the pointer of their mailbox, opened it, and brought out two letters. She knew one was from Ronny. As she was tearing it open, Jan tramped in from the back room, a sack of grain slung over his back. With frank curiosity he peered over her shoulder.

"You get a letter from Ronny?" he asked. "How is he?" A wistful note had crept into Jan's voice.

"He is fine. And he is going to Yale next fall," said Linny. "He wants to come up and see Uncle Truman, Mart, and Jared the first chance he gets."

A warm feeling of pleasure at the prospect of seeing Ronny again flooded through Linny. But it evaporated as soon as they came out of the store and Jan said, "You didn't open your other letter."

She didn't need to. It was addressed to Grandpa, but she knew what it said. It was the tax bill.

Linny drove to Jacksonville in numb despair. After delivering the cream at the creamery she tied Fan to the stone hitching post in Sophronie's yard. She caught sight of Jared's red-checked wool shirt in the big barn. "Jared," she called out, running over the path.

He was pitching hay down from the mow for the cows. When he saw her he put down his pitchfork and waited.

"Oh, Jared, I want to talk to you before I go in the house," she burst out.

"Fire away," he said cheerfully.

Words spilled out of her faster than sparks from a firecracker. She told Jared of Uncle Nat's and Aunt Gloria's wanting to move Grandma and Grandpa to Boston. She told him of the tax bill and that there was no money to pay it.

He leaned on his pitchfork and said, "Well, I never. How about if I come up tonight as soon as I get the chores done? The Nate Chase place has supported farmers for a couple of hundred years. But times are changing."

Mart came to the door and called out to them. "What are you folks doing out there? Linny, come in and have a cup of tea. I haven't seen you in a month of Sundays."

Linny stepped in gladly. Munching Mart's molasses

cookies seemed almost like old times, although it was Sophronie's kitchen. But the baby was fussy with teething, and it was hard to hold a conversation.

When Jared went out with her and untied Fan from the hitching post, she cautioned him, "Don't let on to Grandpa that I told you anything about the fix we're in, will you, Jared? You know how he feels about being beholden to anyone."

Jared promised to keep mum. Linny rattled the whip in the socket and drove home at a good clip, her heart lighter than for many a day. She'd bring up some Baldwins from the cellar and get out Grandma's dandelion wine for Jared.

In no time at all Jared was in the kitchen sitting in a hard straight-backed chair, with the legs tilted back. He chewed on a Baldwin and looked thoughtful. Just to see him there was enough to scare away the dark thoughts that ran through Linny's head.

"Never did see how the timber has grown up in your front pasture, Uncle Newt, and there's quite a few limbs down and some deadwood," Jared said between bites. "On the way up the hill I was thinking maybe you could cut a hundred dollars' or so worth of stove wood and get spot cash for it from Chet Olson down at the Falls."

Grandpa tugged at his beard. "I kinda had the same idea. But who's to cut it? I can't swing an ax no more."

Jared's chair legs came down with a bang. "Land's sakes, Uncle Newt, you know I'd cut it any day in the week," he flared.

"Your time's worth money, ain't it?" Grandpa said, his mouth set in a mulish line. "You git a dollar an hour from summer folks."

Grandma's rockers squeaked over the floorboards. "He's a Chase, ain't he?" she muttered. "A Chase can do for a Chase."

Grandpa's brow furrowed. He seemed to study over it.

"I won't take no for an answer," Jared said firmly. "I'll bring up my chain saw and get that young Polack to help me. We'll start right away."

Linny darted an anxious look at Grandpa's impassive face. Would he let Jared do it? And as for Jan . . . would he let a Pole . . . ?

"Well, I guess you folks got it all settled," Grandpa said, reaching for the bottle. "How about another glass of dandelion wine, Jared? I say nobody can beat Kit makin' dandelion wine."

Grandma's rockers squeaked. She lifted up her lusty old voice in song, her eyes snapping.

"Oh, there's honey in the Rock, my brother,
   There's honey in the Rock for you;
   Leave your sins for the blood to cover,
   There's honey in the Rock for you."

Linny laughed. Grandpa downed his wine. It was merry and warm and bright in the old kitchen.

13

WHEN JAN AND JARED came to cut, Grandpa took Jan into the woodshed and handed him his best flint-edged ax. "I heered you wuz a hard worker, young feller," he said.

The ax rang out merrily in the frosty air. While Jared's chain saw buzzed, Linny helped Jan pile up the wood lengths into Jared's truck. Her heart was full and running over. A hundred dollars, with what they had saved, would pay the taxes.

When the cutting job was done Jan brought the ax into the shed and handed it back to Grandpa.

Grandpa peered down at him from his tall height. "How much do I owe you?"

A queer look came over Jan's face, and Linny's heart stopped. It was the prime tenet of Grandpa's faith not to be beholden, and if he ever suspected Jan knew about the fix they were in, he'd never forgive him, not as long as he lived.

Jan kicked at a shingle. He lifted his dark head, and there was not a flicker of pity in his black eyes, only respect.

"Mr. Storrs," he blurted out, his lean face twisted, "I can still remember what it feels like to have nothing in your stomach. That first winter we came here and near starved to death, it was you folks fed us and gave us seed in the spring. If my pa was alive, he'd beat the hide off me if he ever knew I so much as took a nickel from you."

Grandpa pulled at his beard. His old knotted hand dropped down on Jan's shoulder. "Well, there," he said soothingly, a twinkle in his faded eyes, "I'd say Jan was a true Vermonter, wouldn't you, Linny?"

The taxes were paid before snow came. But winter was on the way. The forested hills blazed their last bright breath and shed a crimson carpet on frosted earth. The sky deepened, and morning found the grasses tipped with white. The woodpile in the yard wore a white rime.

Linny stacked wood in the shed against the coming cold. Strength flowed out of her from some deep inner well. "Land's sakes, if you ain't got more spirit than a Morgan mare," Grandma said.

Fall sharpened into winter. Often the thermometer hovered between twenty and thirty degrees below zero. Snowdrifts were piled three quarters of the way up the kitchen windows. Linny shoveled a path from house to barn for Grandpa, but it was hard for him to do the milking. The cold got into his old bones. Sometimes it stormed so hard they were snowed in and there was no school. Looking up at the deep gray of the snow-laden sky, Linny felt as if even the weather were against them.

In silence Grandpa hobbled around doing his chores, his hands swollen with arthritis, his shoulders lame and sore.

Linny traipsed through the snow uphill and down, carrying Grandma's eggs and butter to houses where workers at the dam lived. But prices were low. It seemed as if the eggs didn't bring enough to buy chicken feed. And there wasn't as much butter as usual.

Grandma was so economical with kerosine that she

never lighted the lamps until it was too dark to see. Grandpa came back from the store without a plug of tobacco in his pocket. They struck rock bottom when the rotting barn floor in one of the stalls gave way and a Jersey stumbled into the hole and broke her leg. The cow had to be butchered, and the loss of Grandma's butter was catastropic. Linny, seventeen now, lay in her bed at night staring into a future darker than a wolf's mouth. If only she could make life easier for the old folks!

Grandma often nagged at her. "Linny, maybe it would be for the best for you to go off down country with Nat and Gloria."

Then Linny would give Grandma's big forearm a poke and say, "Why, Grandma, how you talk! Do you want me to pick up a city slicker for a husband?"

Grandma grinned. "Guess I know which way the wind is blowin'. Well, Jan's a good boy if he is a Polack."

The Poles were making a go of it, Linny thought, turning over in her mind how she might make the Chase farm pay. But Jan's family had his earnings coming in. They also had a tractor and other machinery and Jan's young, strong arms. They were a thrifty family and they all helped out in the fields. And they had given their house a coat of paint inside and out and had laid new floors. Now Jan was talking about putting in electricity and getting a milking machine on credit when the dam was finished.

The dam! If it hadn't been for the dam! Sometimes Linny felt as if their quiet little world had been ripped open by some giant, ruthless hand and she stood on the edge looking down into a black pit. Linny lived with worry. Constantly she was thinking, Where are we going to get the cash to buy another cow? She yearned for spring, but it was months away.

126

January ended in a thaw, and the air became as warm and soft as spring. The sky was blue overhead, but the ground was wet underfoot. Even though it was hard going she welcomed the mud and slogged down the hill in it, headed for the homes of workers at the dam. She had only one pound of butter in her basket and a half dozen eggs. Because they had no money to buy laying mash, the hens weren't laying well. The butter had come from their own table and they had gone without. Never mind, she thought, her spirits rising as she turned into a farmyard, I'll get some tea and molasses at the store before I go home.

At the door the young woman who answered her knock had her hair freshly combed and was dressed in a wool suit instead of the usual housedress.

"Hello, Linny." She reached down into the basket for the golden mound wrapped in waxed paper saved from store bread. "I am afraid you are losing your best customer."

Linny's heart skipped a beat. "Are you leaving town, Mrs. Koski?"

She smiled and nodded her head. "This afternoon. We're going to Texas, and I'll be glad enough to get away from mud for a while."

Linny swallowed hard. "And the others? Are they going too?"

"Why, I suppose so, sooner or later," the woman said briskly. "Work on the dam is slowing up. It will soon be done, and your village will be as empty as a sieve."

Linny clutched the quarter for the butter in her pocket and stumbled back up the hill without stopping at the store or noticing that one of her boots had sprung a leak.

Turning over in her mind what she could do to bring in a little cash, Linny thought of sugaring. When the time came she would stay out of school and help Grandpa collect sap.

Ever since Linny was a child she had felt a sharp delight in tasting the sweet sap as it dripped from the maple trees. She had waded through snowy pastures at Grandpa's heels as he bore the yoke of wooden buckets on his shoulders to the collecting tub drawn by patient Fan. They had turned the sap from the tub into long vats in the sugar house in the woods, and the sap had bubbled merrily for long hours over a wood fire.

When the sap had boiled down the great moment came. Grandpa scooped up some syrup in a pitcher and poured it on a clean snowdrift. As the syrup cooled, the crackling, luscious, sticky sweetness could be wrapped around a fork and thrust cautiously into the mouth for a delectable chew. "Look out, don't break your teeth!" Grandpa always warned. Sugaring was hard work, but it marked the happiest time of the year.

Maple syrup sold readily. With spot cash they could buy another cow so Grandma could make butter to sell. Linny had nailed down some rough boards over the hole in the stall, and it would hold, she hoped.

With the approach of sugar time, with its warm days and cold nights, Linny anxiously eyed the rain clouds hanging over the mountains. The sky looked like a tattered, gray rag. As she climbed out of the school bus at the store on her way home from school, she felt a drop of rain on her face. Old Mose Shawn was lounging on the porch, soberly eyeing Hopping Frog, who was carrying in the mail. She smiled at Mose.

"When you see skunk tracks in the snow, spring's in sight, Linny," old Mose said cheerily.

"Going to be a wet spring and a good hay crop," Jan said as he swung his long legs down. Linny noted that he didn't offer to help Hopping Frog with the mail bags as he used to do for old Mose Shawn.

Linny called out, "Good-bye, Mr. Shawn, good-bye, Jan," and started off up the hill. The snow was melting. Any day now it would be pouring down the sides of the mountains in swollen freshets.

The rains came, washing away the snow and rutting the roads. It was the wettest spring in thirty years. Vermont's raising pond lilies this year, farmers said. The dampness settled into Grandpa's old bones, and it was all he could do to hobble to the barn to tend to his milking. There'll be no sugaring this year, Linny thought sadly. She knew it took thirty-two gallons of sap to make one gallon of maple syrup, and she could never sugar alone. She thought of asking Jared to help, but she knew he was busy with his own sugaring. Besides, they were already under obligation to him for cutting the wood. As for Jan, he was working after school at the Power Company, and she couldn't ask him to help.

Another letter came from Ronny. He was back at school and invited her to the senior prom. It was out of the question, she thought miserably. There was no money for train fare, and she couldn't ask Aunt Gloria for a prom dress . . . not now. Resolutely she put the letter away and made up her mind not to say a word about it to Grandma.

A cloud of despair settled on her that she could not seem to shake off. The day she found the oil can empty of kerosine and the coffee can on the pantry shelf empty of coffee, she thought in a cold misery that she ought to write and tell Uncle Nat about the loss of the cow, Grandpa's arthritis, no sugaring, and one thing piling up on another.

"Ain't no use feelin' bluer than a whetstone," Grandma spluttered. "I ain't forgot how to make tallow candles or how to make coffee out of roasted corn, neither."

Grandpa brought in an ax handle from the woodshed. He had been shaving it out of a piece of clean ash. Now he began sanding it down smooth as paper. "Bet I can get fifty cents for this ax handle, eh, Kit?" he said.

Grandma was busy day in and day out braiding a rug out of rags she had dug out of the attic.

"It's a handsome rug," Linny said in admiration, watching it grow under Grandma's thick fingers, "but who's going to buy it around here?"

A few days later she came home from school to find Grandma in her rocker clutching a five-dollar bill in her hand. "See there, Linny, what'd I tell you!" Grandma clucked in satisfaction.

Linny's eyes widened in amazement. "Grandma, how'd you sell it?"

Grandma chuckled. "Easy as kiss my thumb. All I had to do was ring up Sophronie Chase and ask her did she know anybody wanted to buy a new rag rug, and the whole town, listening in, spread the news. This afternoon up come an engineer's wife from the dam and got it to take with her. They're headin' west for Colorado."

Linny's heart lightened while Grandma rattled on. She made out a grocery list: kerosine, coffee, tea, sugar, salt. . . . But the five dollars wouldn't last long. And then what?

When the lamp was lighted Grandma buried her nose in the *Deerfield Valley Times*. Linny had her books laid out on the red-checked tablecloth and tried to keep her mind on Latin grammar. Scraps of conversations she had heard in the store drifted through her head.

Everyone was talking about the Glory Hole. In zero cold, when mountain winds raked down bearded cheeks like a cross-cut saw, in thunder, hail, and rain, the work at the dam had gone on. Puddled into tight layers by hydraulic pressure, the earth settled harder than concrete. Foot by foot, to towering height, rose the dam. Its crowning achievement blossomed forth, the Morning Glory Hole, a spillway with a walk around its rim and a bridge connecting the spillway with the control tower.

"See the Morning Glory Hole," shouted the official guide of the Power Company when awe-struck tourists flocked in. "Only one in the world made by man, and a copy of Old Glory in Yellowstone Park. Five hundred and eight feet in circumference, sixty feet in diameter at the mouth, one hundred eighty-six feet deep, twenty-six feet in diameter at the base. It will empty into a by-pass tunnel thirteen hundred feet in length and spill into the lower side of the dam."

The dam seemed to intrude into every corner of Linny's life. One day as she climbed Chase Hill on her way home from school, she heard a familiar voice behind her calling, "Linny."

A little seed of hope sprang up in her out of the darkness as she turned and watched Jan push up the hill toward her. He swung to a stop and dug at the dirt in the road with the toe of his sneaker, his hands thrust into the pockets of his jeans.

Linny moved a step toward him, looking forward to taking a walk with him as they used to do. She would take her sketch pad, and they would sit on a stone wall, and if the sun came out she'd sketch, not saying anything, just knowing he was there beside her, understanding how she felt.

"Linny," he said. He raised his head and excitement shone in his eyes. "I've got a half day off from the Power Company. You ought to come with me and see what's going on down at the dam. They've got a crane down there that was used in building the Panama Canal. And the Glory Hole—it's a sight, I can tell you. If you could see the Glory Hole it might make you feel better about the dam."

Linny whirled on her heels and plunged up the road. She knew he must be standing there staring after her, his eyes hurt and wondering. But she kept on blindly stumbling up the hill.

14.

Mud time is a season in Vermont. Wet spring skies turn roads into rivers of mud. Wagon wheels sink axle deep, and going uphill or down in a car is fraught with peril. Farm women scold as they spread newspapers on clean kitchen floors to catch the mud from menfolks' rubber boots.

"Land's sakes, spring's come," Grandma said the day Grandpa tracked in a trail of mud. She toiled up the attic to stare at rows of empty bottles, piles of old newspapers, hoarded string, and other odds and ends. "I declare, Linny, we better throw out all this truck," she said, same as every spring, and then she went back downstairs to rock placidly by the window and let sleeping dogs lie. Linny kept most of the mud swept out.

Making her way home from school over the muddy roads one day, Linny heard the sound of a hammer ring out at the foot of Chase Hill. She turned in the yard, and there was Uncle Truman with his mouth full of nails hammering a board over the kitchen window. Just the other day she had met him as he was limping down the road, his face sunken. He had stopped her and said, "Linny, why don't you come to see me no more?" Since Jared and Mart and the baby had moved to Jacksonville, she thought guiltily, she hadn't set foot in the house.

She came up softly now and stood beside him. When he saw her he thrust his hammer in his pocket and took the nails out of his mouth. "Well, Linny, I thought you'd plumb forgot me."

She saw that the woodpile was all gone. Only a few scattered shavings littered the yellowed grass where it had been. The barn doors were shut tight.

He fitted a board neatly over a window. "Ain't no use boardin' up. The Power Company will probably burn the house down. But I'm doin' it anyways."

Through the half-boarded-up window Linny could see the spot where Mart used to sit in her rocker and cut up apples for pies.

"Mose Shawn's got all our stuff in his barn," Truman went on. "I can't see myself settin' in Sophronie Chase's barn of a house. I'm a-goin' away, Linny. Vermont winters don't do my old bones no good. I'm a-goin' to Florida, sit in the sun, and do a little fishin'."

Florida! Linny thought numbly of Mart's finger traveling across the map of South America.

"Folks here will think I got a screw loose." He swung his hammer and drove in a nail with one blow.

Pointing to a bulky brown paper bundle at his feet, he said, "Mart wanted you should have that. I was goin' to bring it up to you."

She leaned down and tore a corner of the paper and saw that it was Great-Grandmother Betsy's log-cabin quilt.

"There's something I want you should do for me, Linny. Mart's busy with the baby and still gettin' settled. I want you should write to Ronny about us losing the place and Mart movin' to Jacksonville."

Linny nodded wordlessly. Her tounge felt like it was hitched to an iron post.

He looked down at her, and she saw the furrows

ground deep in his old face. "Don't let on to Kit that I'm a-goin' away. I'll come up and tell her when I'm ready, in a day or two. Likely it'll scare her that she'll be the next one to lose out. But 'tain't always so. She'll be glad to know the Power Company's changed its mind about wantin' Cousin Joe Tainter's Brick House. And him ready to sign the deed!"

When Linny told Grandma about the Brick House being saved she rocked vigorously and cracked her thumbs. "There!" she said. "Sometimes things work out by leaving well enough alone."

But the Brick House being saved didn't do Cousin Joe any good. One frosty morning the Italian from Readsboro on his grocery route found Cousin Joe lying in the middle of his kitchen floor.

"Died with his boots on and him ninety years old," townsfolk said proudly, and they bragged about how to the last day he had cooked his own meals and swept his own floors.

"Joe never had no more get-up-and-go than a lizard," Grandma said plaintively, getting into her best black for the funeral. "But he never sulked in his life."

"Joe always made danged good cider," Grandpa said, tying his black tie.

"Cousin Joe taught me a lot about nature," Linny added, her eyes stinging.

Man, woman, and child, the whole town turned out for Joe's laying away, and everyone had a good word for him.

Even Uncle Nat and Aunt Gloria, who came up from Boston for the funeral, had approval to spare for Cousin Joe. "He kept that old house in apple-pie order," said Gloria.

She opened up her suitcase and took out a green wool dress with colored embroidery at the neck. "Black isn't suitable for a seventeen-year-old," she said. "I thought you could do with a new dress, Linny."

Linny thanked her and slid the dress over her head, feeling strange in its luxurious softness. She couldn't help thinking how many groceries the price of such a dress would have bought. If only she could tell Aunt Gloria and Uncle Nat about their plight! But if she did they would only push harder for them all to move down country.

Already Grandma and Aunt Gloria were arguing. Aunt Gloria, who was standing in front of the kitchen mirror applying lipstick, said, "I don't see what difference it makes where you're buried. When you're gone, you're gone."

Grandma, ready for the funeral and waiting in her rocker, tapped her cane nervously against the floorboards. "All our folks been laid away in Sugar Hill Cemetery since the Revolution. Deliverance Tainter, Nathan and Betsy Chase, all the Chases since the first Nathan and Abigail," Grandma said.

Grandpa, who was pacing restlessly around the room, stopped and rested a gaunt elbow on the window ledge by Grandma. He shifted his broad-brimmed black felt hat to the back of his white head. "Well, there won't be no more Chases buried in Sugar Hill Cemetery now the Power Company's moved the stones," he said.

Linny's heart jumped. No, they wouldn't lay Cousin Joe under the wild long grass among the thin old stones blackened by wind and rain. She thought of Mart swinging along Sugar Hill Cemetery with her easy stride, her blackberry pail hanging from her belt, the sun on her hair. Cousin Joe would have to make do with the new cemetery the Power Company had laid out. The fresh graves were covered with naked loam where not a green blade sprouted. And the cemetery was right across the road from the new filling station where, in a flurry of mud, the trucks came to fill their tanks.

Uncle Nat, in a navy-blue suit and black hat, slouched against the kitchen doorjamb, his hands in his pockets. "It takes you folks up here fifty years to get used to a new idea. Someday you'll be pointing out the new cemetery to visitors and bragging about it. You'll say what a fine job the Power Company did moving the bodies up from Sugar Hill and how it didn't cost the village a cent."

Grandma stopped rocking and her tongue clicked. "Well, let's git goin'," she said. "What has to be has to be."

It was a sad day, but it came to an end. That night Linny lingered in the parlor bedroom watching Gloria fold her black chiffon in tissue paper and tuck it into her suitcase. She listened to Gloria's light voice and the silken swish of her skirts. If only she could unlock her tongue and tell Aunt Gloria how things were!

"Linny, run out and get my stockings off the line, will you, darling?" Gloria asked.

Linny ran out of the room on swift feet, glad to do even a little thing. Outside in the dark she unpinned the stockings from the line. Through the open window of the parlor bedroom she caught the sound of Gloria's voice muffled with anger as she talked to Uncle Nat.

"So now Mart is saddled with Sophronie Chase," she said. "It's a crying shame. She ought to have got out of here years ago. I tried to tell her."

Uncle Nat's voice came thick and blurred. "Mart always was one to put her neck in a noose."

"Maybe Uncle Truman's selling out will help to move things along," Gloria said. "The old folks can't be making out too well. Someday they'll have to give in. They can't hold out forever."

Linny could hear Gloria's light sigh. "Better not say anything tonight, Nat. Now is not the time. But I wish we could get Linny away from here. She is so stubborn, and they'll back her to the hilt. Sometimes I think we made a mistake in ever sending her up here to the backwoods."

Linny stood on frozen feet, her ankles chilled and wet. She looked up at the stars bright over the black hulk of Haystack. The quiet branches of the maples loomed up in silence against the dark sky. She could not imagine leaving the country!

When Linny stepped into the kitchen Uncle Nat was sitting in one of the hard straight chairs. His round shoulders were bent forward, and the palms of his hands moved restlessly up and down his thighs.

"The way I look at it, folks," he was saying, "Uncle Truman's right lucky. That land fronting the river isn't worth a straw, and you know it."

"Who asked your advice?" Grandma demanded bluntly from her rocker, pounding her cane on the floor.

Gloria came to the door. Her face looked white and tired. "Now what's the fuss about? Nat and I have to go back in the morning, and goodness knows it's been a hard day for all of us. Can't we have one peaceful evening?"

"Uncle Nat, there's some blackberry jam, and I'll make some toast and coffee," Linny said, handing Gloria her stockings.

"Guess that would set about right," Grandpa murmured.

Gloria flashed Linny a grateful glance. But as Linny moved toward the stove her arms and legs felt numb.

Uncle Nat scowled and drummed his fingers on the table. But when the fragrant coffee was poured into

Betsy's cottage china cups and the thick jam was set out, Nat's tense face relaxed.

"Linny," he said, biting into his second piece of homemade bread, "when there's anything you want, you just write and tell your Uncle Nat."

Linny's throat filled. "Uncle Nat . . ." she began. But the words wouldn't come.

After Uncle Nat and Aunt Gloria were gone, an empty stillness seemed to settle over the land. The mountains were lost in fog for days at a time, and the fields were shrouded in clouds of mist.

One gray Saturday morning, leaning listlessly on her broom handle, Linny saw through the kitchen window John Link climbing Chase Hill with the slow, easy gait of the mountaineer. She knew why he had come, and she knew that Grandma knew when she showed him in. He sat down in Grandpa's chair and took his pipe out of his pocket.

Grandma pushed onto the back of the stove the pan of sour milk that was thickening for cottage cheese and sat down in her rocker by the window.

"Calista," Mr. Link said, puffing on his pipe, "your headpiece is fastened on tight. You knew plumb well Truman was beat. Why don't you give in now and save us all some trouble?"

Grandma rocked as if she were going to a fire. "How come they let the Brick House go?" she demanded.

Link shifted his long legs. "They don't need to go up that far for a watershed. I'm sorry about your cousin Joe. I'm not feelin' so good about takin' things up with you so soon after Joe is in the ground, but that Mr. Wells has been pesterin' me."

"There's the law," Grandma said testily. "A home owner can fight in court for his rights."

Link smoked in silence. The thin line of his mouth and the thin line of his brows were like set in flint. "Kit, that don't go no more. Time was when a body could fight it out. Today's different. You can't go agin a corporation."

Grandma's eyes flashed fire. "By what rights can they do me out of land that is rightfully mine in the eyes of the law?" she snapped.

Link took his pipe out of his mouth and leaned forward. He spoke slowly and distinctly. "They can take it by right of eminent domain. A company that can prove it is making a public improvement for the good of all can force any landowner to sell. That's the law."

Grandma's mouth twitched. "Ain't this a free country?" she stormed.

Her words fell back from the granite surface of Link's weathered face like pebbles shied against a concrete wall. "It won't do you no good to be stubborn as a mule. It ain't worth it. Calista; you can't fight twenty million dollars with the proceeds from a couple of cows."

Grandma rubbed her apron over the misted window. "Land's sakes, fog's thick. Can't see a foot ahead of you." Her heavy shoulders lunged around. "Where in tunket did I put my eyeglasses?"

She heaved up out of her chair, and like a ship in a forward wind labored across the room. Linny saw Grandma's glasses lying behind the clock on the shelf and handed them to her silently.

"And what do you get out of this, John Link?" Grandma demanded.

He grinned and uncrossed his bony legs. He reached in his vest pocket for some papers and began to rummage through them. "I see to it the Power Company don't cheat me none," he said.

A slow light ripened in Grandma's eyes. "And collect

from both sides. I vum!" She scowled down at him from heavy brows. "That Mr. Wells and me wouldn't see eye to eye in a hundred years, but he is what he is—a feller what knows which side of the fence he's on and willin' to pay for it. While you . . . you ain't neither one of us nor one of them."

"Nope," he agreed. "I'm lookin' out for number one."

Grandma's voice trembled in scorn. "Ain't no lower critter under the sky than him what stands up for nothin'," she thundered.

"Pshaw," Grandpa said from the doorway, "what you spittin' at?"

Linny fled to the chicken coop and began gathering the eggs.

After Mr. Link left, Linny trudged down to the store. There was no money to buy groceries. She leaned against the counter waiting for the mail. When it came, there was nothing but the *Deerfield Valley Times*. Black headlines were plastered across the front page: BIG EARTH DAM BUILT IN SADAWGA SPRINGS.

She folded up the paper without reading any more and went out. A heavy truck rumbled up to the new filling station in a swirl of mud. Across the road workers were busy raking the bald graves in the new cemetery.

At the foot of Chase Hill Linny stopped to look upriver at a sparkling reservoir stretching back twelve miles to Wilmington. She still couldn't get used to the sight of clear water lapping at the new shore where Mart's house had once stood. Water flowed over Sugar Hill Cemetery and over the spot where the old station had been. The nearest railroad station was now fifteen miles away at the Falls.

Familiar landmark after familiar landmark had disappeared. Gone was the old Bratton house, the oldest house in town, which had been built in the days of the

French and Indian Wars. The elderly Bratton sisters had left weeping. And gone was the Trim place. One-armed Holland Trim had been the last to leave. With his one arm hooked around an old musket, he had met the Power Company workers at the door when they came to burn his house down.

"As if he could stop us! That old gun must have dated from before the Civil War," one of the workers had said, laughing as he told about it afterward in the store. Holland Trim had gone with the rest of the old folks . . . no one knew where. . . .

The village roads were deserted. No longer did Linny meet foreign-looking faces on the roads. Irish, Italian, French-Canadian—they had drained out of town as swiftly as they had come. The door of the log cabin swung on its hinges. Inside, the bar was empty. On the shores of Lake Sadawga no thin wisps of smoke trailed up from board shacks. No sound of pounding engines vibrated through the still air. The dam was finished.

Linny turned her eyes away from the strange new sights. Nothing, she thought, would ever be the same again.

15.

THE SHACKS had disappeared from the shores of Lake Sadawga like a bad dream at morning. Spring green covered the bare spots where they had stood, and once more lush meadow flowed to the edge of the lake. The log cabin was torn down and the old springhouse replaced, with new latticework and a new pump. On the banks of the Deerfield River waved the feathery green of newly planted pine.

As water tumbled through the sluiceways, "white coal" was mined at the powerhouse. Generators throbbed, switches were thrown, and transformers stepped up electricity to 220,000 volts. Transmission lines hummed. The power was on.

Poles were set and wires strung and, in farmhouses on isolated hills and in the village hollow, oil lamps flickered and went out for the last time. Light bloomed at the touch of a button. Wooden washtubs were carried out to the barn and gleaming white machines turned out a morning's wash in half an hour. Heavy flatirons were stored in the attic. The old wooden ice box, the wood-burning range, and the hand lantern disappeared. Cows were milked under the glare of an electric bulb, and large herds were milked by machine. After chores were done the farmer pulled off his boots, drew up his rocker to the radio, and gave ear to the outside world. The hands of the clock moved forward in Sadawga Springs.

There was talk of a new schoolhouse to serve both Sadawga Springs and Jacksonville. It would stand halfway between the two villages, and the children would be bused to school. The town hired an architect to design a modern building accommodating children from kindergarten through high school. There would be a gymnasium, sunny classrooms, a library, a kitchen, and a cafeteria.

Linny stopped in front of the school bulletin board for a look at the architect's drawings.

"Pretty spiffy for Sadawga Springs," said Jan, coming up beside her. He acted as if nothing had ever happened between them, as if she had not run off and left him on the hill that day. Linny was thankful and willing to forget the rift, although she still felt hurt inside.

"If it weren't for the tax money from the Power Company, Sadawga Springs would never get such a school," Jan pointed out.

Linny stiffened. "We'll never agree on the Power Company," she snapped. "If it was your house they wanted to buy, maybe you'd feel different."

Jan laughed. "My ma would have sold out at the drop of a hat, and glad enough to get the cash," Jan persisted. "Linny, let's forget about the Power Company. Let's have a good time at the senior prom. After all, we only graduate once." His eyes pleaded with her. She knew how hard he had worked and how little fun he had had lately.

Linny relented. "I'd like some fun too," she said.

For a brief time Linny made herself shut out dark thoughts. Aunt Gloria sent her a new dress for the prom, with a note saying she and Uncle Nat were too busy to come now but they would be up later. She begged Linny to think again about going to college. Enclosed was a check for twenty-five dollars, a graduation gift. The check was more than welcome, and Linny put it aside toward another Jersey cow.

The dress of soft blue silk had a full, ankle-length skirt, a tight bodice, and tiny cap sleeves. Linny felt like Cinderella when she put it on the night of the dance. She clasped Great-Grandmother Betsy's gold beads around her neck, combed her shoulder-length hair smooth, and went to show herself to Grandma.

"Land's sakes, if you ain't the spittin' image of Betsy Chase," Grandma boomed. "Don't let it turn your head!"

At the dance Linny sparkled as she twirled from one partner to the next. She wished the music would go on forever and that she never had to come to grips with unsolved problems.

Jan drove her home in an ancient Ford he had bought and tinkered with to get it into running shape. Happily they discussed the evening's excitement, until Jan said, "This summer the Power Company's giving me a better job and a raise."

Always the Power Company, Linny thought, feeling her pleasure in the evening ooze away. She wished she could wake up and find it was all a bad dream.

Grandma was waiting up for her, and she had to crowd down the dark thoughts and give her a full account of the evening.

"A Chase always likes a good time," Grandma said happily, and off to bed she hobbled.

After the prom Linny counted the days that were left of school. She couldn't bear to have school over with; she had had a happy four years in the shabby, overcrowded schoolhouse. But soon she'd have to make up her mind what to do, because Uncle Nat and Aunt Gloria were pressing her.

On graduation night a lump crept into her throat as her class marched up to the platform while the school band played "Pomp and Circumstance." She strained to catch a glimpse of Mart and Jared, who had brought Grandma and Grandpa to see her graduate. If she went away to college, how would the old folks get along without her?

Seated on the platform waiting for her diploma, Linny was proud of Jan as he stood in front of the lectern and gave the valedictorian address. He was the smartest one in the class. He was the one who should be going away to college, and he would be if it weren't for the Power Company. "Someday I'll be superintendent," he had said. "You'll see." She made up her mind to have another talk with Jan in the hope he would change his mind about going to college.

But after graduation Jan was so busy at the Power Company that he paid scant attention to Linny's urging. "The Power Company's training me," he said. "My work is as good as a college education."

Linny gave up. With the rest of the villagers she turned her attention to the swift influx of summer people. Every hillside grew a summer place. A hit song writer named Goldstein from New York's Tin Pan Alley bought the Brick House from Cousin Joe's nephew. He scoured the country for antiques and topped most of the bids at auctions.

Knocks sounded on farmhouse doors. Polite voices with New York accents inquired about homemade butter and fresh eggs. Linny's spirits brightened when she bought a Jersey calf with the twenty-five dollars Gloria had sent her for graduation plus cash from eggs

146

and berries. Linny's fingers were dyed purple and her bare legs raked by wild bushes. She sold all she could pick of lush raspberries, blueberries, and early garden truck, but the money came in driblets and would not be enough for the taxes, which were due again in the fall. Linny wished she were a man and could carpenter like Jared, who had all the work he could take care of.

Sophronie called Grandma and said Jared had bought Mart an electric washing machine and that saved a lot of work with the baby.

"My land," Grandma said, "how much is the power costin' you?"

Then a notice came from the selectmen. Since the Power Company would pay ninety percent of the town taxes, the rates had been reduced. The dream of a farmer's life had come miraculously true. This fall taxes would be cut in half.

Grandpa looked as if he had seen the sun come up in the west. He scratched his head, folded up his long legs in a kitchen chair, and read the letter again and again.

"I got to study over it," he said, tugging at his beard.

"I swan," Grandma said, "I wish we could set a few poles for electricity."

Linny's spirits brightened. She sat down to figure. Grandpa never kept books, never knew where he stood. It would help to keep a record and to learn to do things the new way. What about the old apple orchard? She poured over bulletins from the U.S. Department of Agriculture.

"Pshaw, book farmin'," Grandpa said, and stuck to his almanac.

Linny decided that to bring back the orchard would take expensive spraying equipment and skilled grafting, and that in the end they still couldn't compete with the lush product of down-country apple growers.

But there were berries. Summer folks loved berries, and there were never enough—even for the villagers. No one in town raised berries. Farm wives picked them wild to can for the table. Folks would think she had a screw loose if she tried to cultivate berries. Black Caps, Royal Purple, Cardinal—she mooned over varieties advertised in the catalogs. Raspberries didn't need much care. She could sell them in the village and down country too.

She sent to Amherst for more catalogs. Maybe next winter she could go to agricultural school for a few weeks.

Things were moving ahead in town, too. They had the Grange and the Co-operative Creamery now. Farmers were learning to band together and help one another.

Linny was so busy she hardly missed the professor's girls who had not come up this summer. But at last she had a letter from Marilyn saying they were all three going to a summer camp. In the fall Marilyn would enter Smith College. How about Linny? she asked. What was she going to do?

Linny sighed and tucked the letter away in her top bureau drawer. Her main concern now was to save enough to take care of the taxes in the fall.

One morning she got up to see gray skies threatening rain. That would mean no berry picking. Nor could she pick the next day if a good rain ruined the crop.

Sure enough, the rain came, pouring day and night without stopping. On the second day torrents hurried down the mountainsides. Brooks rose and rushed pell-mell toward the Deerfield River. Grandma peered uneasily out the kitchen window. "Land's sakes, ain't seen such a rain since the flood of 1927," she said.

"Pshaw," Grandpa said, and emptied a trail of milk

pans he had set under new leaks the roof had sprung.

Linny wandered restlessly around the house. Now was a good time to write to Ronny, as she had promised Uncle Truman. She ought to tell him about Uncle Truman's losing his house to the Power Company and about Mart's and Jared's moving to Jacksonville. She owed Marilyn a letter too.

She sat down at the round dining-room table and tried to put words together, but they turned out stiff and formal. Both Ronny and Marilyn seemed far away and like strangers. With an effort she finished the letters.

The rain never stopped. On the third day Linny pulled on her rubber boots, struggled into Grandpa's old slicker and his brown felt hat, and slogged downhill to mail her letters.

In the store there was no one around except Hal Eames, his white apron as starched as ever, his horrid smile glued on.

"Nasty day," he said cheerfully. "The mail isn't in yet."

After posting her letters Linny huddled in the corner by the mailboxes, water trickling down her neck from the brim of Grandpa's hat, her boots muddying the clean floor.

The door burst open, and old Mose Shawn stomped in, his head lowered like a bull, his heavy shoulders splattering rain in all directions. "Crimus, what a load of rain!" he shouted.

Hard on his heels pounded a stranger in an English tweed coat, a gray fedora pulled down toward his nose. Hal Eames eyed him respectfully.

"A package of Luckies and a Boston *Post*," the stranger said in a pleasant voice, flipping some coins on the counter.

Linny's heart leaped to her throat. Was there something familiar in that voice?

Now he turned to old Mose, and she recognized the curve of his pink, freshly shaven cheek. It was Mr. Wells from the Power Company!

Old Mose squinted at him. "Where be you from, stranger?"

"East, west, north, and south," he answered good-naturedly, as his plump hands tore open the cellophane on the cigarettes.

He turned on his heels and his eyes fell full on Linny. "Aren't you from up on Chase Hill?" he asked.

"Yes," she answered in a strangled voice. "My grandmother is Mrs. Storrs."

"Tell your grandmother I'll be up to see her in a day or two," he said. "I'm having car trouble, and I'll be held up until my car is repaired. How's your hill? Muddy?"

Her legs began to shake. "Yes, it is," she said.

Not waiting for Hopping Frog and the mail, she pushed her way blindly out of the store and stumbled up the hill. Rain was streaming down her face and the mud sucked at her boots. As she slogged up the road she muttered to herself, If he tries to make Chase Hill, I hope he gets stuck.

16.

THE NEXT DAY it still rained, a thick, sodden downpour. Anxiously Linny looked out the kitchen window, but there was no sign of the stranger's car. Likely he was waiting for the weather to clear. She didn't mention to Grandma that she had seen the man in the store.

Grandma scrubbed at a windowpane with her apron and muttered darkly, "Ain't a fittin' day for man nor beast. Newt, you'd best give up going to Jacksonville today."

"Pshaw," Grandpa said, "can't let more than a gallon of cream sour."

"You stay home, Grandpa," Linny pleaded. "The damp will get into your bones, and you'll be so crippled you can't milk. I can take over the cream."

But Grandpa was like a rock. "Can't never tell what'll happen in weather like this," he said.

Linny pulled on an old coat. She climbed into the buggy beside Grandpa and opened up the big carriage umbrella.

On the way to Jacksonville she sat silent, hardly aware of the steaming rain. They delivered the cream and started back. Suddenly Linny realized that the sky was getting to be as dark as night and that the pounding rain was churning the road into ankle-deep mud. As the buggy rattled across a wooden bridge she looked back fearfully at the brook, which was swollen from four days of rain. The rising waters were tearing at the bridge abutments. A gust of wind swept in under the big carriage umbrella. She lowered the umbrella in its socket and tried to hold it against the savage wind. Only a mile to Sadawga Springs now. . . .

"Don't like the looks of that sky," Grandpa muttered, and slapped the reins over Fan's rump.

The wind was blowing a gale. The roadside brush twisted and writhed and gave up its last leaves. The sky had become a queer mustard color with streaks of brass in it. With sudden fury the wind swirled down, and away went the umbrella, fluttering over the meadow like a leaf. Loud sounds like the popping of guns burst in the air. Linny had a confused glimpse of huge maples and firs toppling like toothpicks.

"Git out!" Grandpa shouted. He sprang over the wheel and began tugging at Fan's harness.

In one leap Linny flew over the shafts into the mud of the road. Her trembling fingers fumbled with the harness buckles. And not a moment too soon. The wind snatched up the loosened buggy as if it were a feather and tossed it into the ditch, where it was smashed to smithereens. There was a roar from behind. Linny whipped around as she saw the bridge they had crossed hardly five minutes ago collapsing in a shamble of boards. The gentle little brook had become a raging torrent.

"Grab holt of Fan and stick!" Grandpa yelled in her ear.

Fan was shaking like a leaf. The water was halfway to her gambrels. The roar of the river mingled with the din of crashing trees and the shrieking wind. Wreckage whirled through the air. Down in the boiling waters a chicken house plunged past, the chickens flapping their wings on tumbling boards. Ahead rose the roof of the Links' barn. Linny clutched Fan's bridle and pressed her body against the wind. Only a few hundred yards to the Links'. Could they make it?

The rain lashed against their faces like knives. The wind whipped their legs and backs, beating them back every step they took. The Link house seemed miles away. Fear ran along Linny's veins like quicksilver. This wind would sweep across Chase Hill, and an old house with loose clapboards would be less than an eggshell in its grip. And Grandma there all alone. Linny groaned inwardly. Why had they ever come out on such a day?

A huge elm crashed at the side of the road, and Fan jumped and reared. Linny hung to the bridle with a strangle grip. Only a few more steps now.

The wind was like a wall. She pushed against it with all her strength, her breath draining from her lungs, coming out in little gasps. They slogged into the driveway in a crazy, drunken stagger. Grandpa unloosed her numb fingers, shoved her toward the house, and headed for the barn with Fan. Linny stumbled up onto the porch, her arms blindly outspread to find the door. An ear-splitting crash sounded right at her heels.

"Grandpa!" she screamed. She whirled around.

Prone across the driveway, its torn roots clawing the air, lay a giant maple in the spot where a minute ago Grandpa had stood with Fan. Looking at the tangle of branches, Linny began to sob and shake all over. But the barn doors stood open. Grandpa had made it.

Mrs. Link swung open the front door. "Jumpin' Jehoshaphat! Linny!" she cried. "What are you doing out in a hurricane?"

Linny's knees wobbled like the legs of a young lamb as

Mrs. Link pulled off her wet coat, rubbed her chilled hands, and helped her into a chair by the kitchen stove. "There," she crooned, "a good hot cup of tea will fix you up."

"I've got to call Grandma." Linny tried to struggle to her feet.

Mrs. Link laid a hand on her shoulder. "Bless you, child, the phone went out first lick. All lines are down. But don't you worry none about Calista. She'll make out."

Grandpa stomped in dripping like a wet bear, his breath coming out in bursts. "Lost the buggy, but got the hoss in safe," he gasped. "Link, I tied my hoss in your barn. Must be a hundred-mile-an-hour gale."

Link, sitting in his rocker with his ear glued tight to the radio, tilted up his scrawny neck. Sweat stood out on his forehead. His eyes seemed to be bursting from his head.

"Hell's a-poppin' all right, Newt. It swept clear the length of New England, from all reports. Cut a hundred-and-fifty-mile swath through Rhode Island, Connecticut, Massachusetts, Vermont, and New Hampshire. All along the lines roads are blocked, bridges washed out, and railroads catchin' Ned. Just heard the whole side of Negus Mountain moved down on a line of freight and dumped twenty cars in the Deerfield."

Linny's pleading eyes went to Grandpa. "Do you suppose Grandma is all right?" she whispered hoarsely.

He sank into a kitchen chair and spread out his legs. "I aim to find out soon's I git my breath."

Mrs. Link picked up a teapot. "Newt, you have a cup of tea before you set foot in that inferno."

Linny cradled a hot cup in her hand while Grandpa sipped his tea. The windows rattled as if they would burst. It was black as night outside. The voice from the radio went briskly on. "Reports have come in that fire has broken out in the business district of Peterboro, but all communications have now been cut. All roads are blocked. . . ."

The electric lights flickered and went out. The darkness outside reached in and licked them up like a dog's tongue. The voice on the radio went abruptly silent.

"Power's off," Link said. He rose from his chair, went to a window, and stood listening.

Through the uproar of the wind, out of the dark, came the faint, far-off tolling of a bell.

"It's the church bell," Mrs. Link said, and in the dim light Linny saw her hands open and close mechanically.

Link and Grandpa stared at each other. "Git me one of your shovels, Link," Grandpa said, and struggled to his feet.

Link was already headed for the woodshed. Mrs. Link took down a kerosine lamp from the shelf and lighted it. "First time the power's gone off," she said shakily. A line of white circled her mouth. Her eyes were deep, dark pools.

Link came in with two shovels, threw them down, and began pulling on his overcoat.

Grandpa picked up one of the shovels, but Linny leaped from her chair and clutched his sleeve. "Grandpa, where are you going?"

Grandpa's face was as stern as flint. "That bell means trouble, Linny. If'n that dam goes out, it'll flood the valley clear down through Connecticut and wash through every town and city on the way."

"And leave ruin behind it," Link said grimly, picking up the other shovel. "There wouldn't be nothin' left of

Greenfield, Northampton, Holyoke, Springfield. . . .
Once it gets started, there'll be no stoppin' it. Do more
damage than an army."

Linny's face turned paper white. "But Grandma . . ."
she whimpered.

"There ain't no choice, Linny." Mrs. Link thrust a
stick of wood in the stove and turned the damper. "If
the dam goes it'll make kindling out of hundreds of
homes and take the lives of women and children. Every
man will be needed at the dam. Your grandma will hear
the church bell and know how it has to be."

She tied a wool scarf around her head and buttoned
on an old coat. "If all the menfolks in town head for the
dam, I reckon there'll be women needed to help out at
the hospital and prepare victuals in the church vestry,"
she murmured.

Link and Grandpa were already at the door. "Linny,
you stay here," Grandpa demanded. "This old house is
solid and tight and protected from the wind by a side
hill."

"No, wait!" Linny cried, scrambling into her wet coat
and cap.

Mrs. Link's mouth flattened into a thin line. "There
ain't no place that's safe, Newt," she said. She blew out
the lamp and tucked Linny's hand through her arm.
"Hang tight, Linny," she said. "The wind ain't never
blowed me away yet."

Outside, the sky was rolling with pitching black
clouds. The brook was churning up mountainous
waves. In the dim light Linny saw that the water was full
of boards. A dog swept past and then a cow on her back,
her legs waving in the air like wooden sticks. Linny
clung to Mrs. Link as they plowed through the mud,
fighting the wind inch by inch. As they rounded the
corner by the store, the wind gripped them in a frenzied

clutch, and they were almost blown onto the empty stage, which was lying on its side in the road.

"Guess Hopping Frog got his!" Grandpa shouted.

A vision of a round, sleek head, stiff hair, and tight lips floated through Linny's head. Hopping Frog, who never waited for anyone, where was he now?

"There's a road truck from the Power Company at the store, Newt," Link bawled, his stiff old legs quickening their pace. "And there's the community rescue wagon in front of the hospital."

Jared must be on duty, Linny thought hopefully, for he was chief of the rescue team. If he was in the hospital she could tell him about Grandma. A second later she spied Jan among the men milling around on the porch of the store, all carrying shovels, axes, coils of rope, and burlap bags. Jan had a shovel in one hand, and his eyes blazed with excitement. Breaking away from Mrs. Link, Linny battled her way across the road and shouted in Jan's ear, "What's happened down at the dam?"

He scowled down at her. "For Pete's sake, Linny, what are you doing out in a hurricane?"

She shook his arm with impatience. "Jan, tell me about the dam."

"The Glory Hole's full," he said. "The wind's shooting water over the top of the dam. They're piling up sandbags on the levee, trying to hold it back."

Men were piling into the truck. There was old Mose Shawn in his mackinaw and felt cap, old Mr. Butterfield, two Poles, looking short and small-boned beside the tall, gaunt Vermonters. There were even some summer people. That Mr. Goldstein from Tin Pan Alley, who had bought the Brick House, was holding a shovel like the others. Now Link and Grandpa climbed into the truck. All of them, drenched and pounded by rain, hurled raucous shouts into the darkness.

Mrs. Link stood beside Linny, watching. "Ain't it a pity," she said thoughtfully, "that human critters can't git along all the time the way they can when they got their necks in the same noose."

Suddenly, cutting through all that noise, an easy, pleasant voice said clearly, "Can you use a greenhorn?"

It was the stranger. In his pearl-gray fedora, his light oxfords, and his tweed coat among the men with their rubber hip boots, windbreakers and caps, he stood out like a single blackberry in a dish of cream.

"What good will he be down there?" Linny cried, clutching Jan's arm. "He won't know how to handle himself any better than a youngster on a state highway."

The stranger had heard her. He looked up, smiled, and waved. "I can shovel sand," he said, looking at his soft, plump hands.

"Come on up, stranger," old Mose yelled. "What in tarnation you waitin' for?"

"Git him some rubber boots in the store," someone shouted. Long arms reached down and helped him up into the truck, and Mr. Butterfield handed him some boots.

Jan's fingers dug deep into Linny's arm. "Now don't be a fool and try to get home," he warned. "Not over that thick wood road."

"All hands on deck," shouted old Mose, and the truck snorted and throbbed.

Jan grabbed Linny and pressed her close to his wet leather jacket. His lips quickly touched her cheek, and then he leaped across the porch and swung himself upon the truck, lithe as a cat.

Linny stood watching, one hand cupped over her cheek where Jan had kissed her.

A furious gust shattered the glass of the store windows. The porch boards shook underfoot. Mud showered up from grinding wheels. The truck swayed, skidded, and plunged on its way.

"Good-bye," she called out, and waved, standing close to Mrs. Link. She strained her eyes to catch a last glimpse through the driving rain of Grandpa's white beard and Jan's dark face.

The truck nosed on. Now it had rounded the bend. Her throat tightened. All that stood between roaring waters bearing death and destruction for hundreds of miles was that little handful of men.

"Come, Linny," Mrs. Link said briskly. "Let's git to work."

Once more they bent their shoulders to the wind and fought their way across the road to the hospital. As they passed the rescue wagon, Mrs. Link said, "Someone must have been injured."

17
.

INSIDE THE SMALL HOSPITAL the blinds were closed against the wind, and the long front room was in darkness where the lamplight did not reach. A row of cots had been added to the few hospital beds, and most of them were filled with patients lying on top of the blankets with their clothes still on. Other patients sat in chairs nursing their injuries while waiting their turn.

In the feeble flicker of a lantern set on a table Linny saw the slim figure of young Doc Adams bent over a child. A woman moaned from the shadows beyond, and Mrs. Adams, in the white uniform of a nurse, said softly, "We'll get to you in just a minute now."

Linny caught sight of Jared leaning over a still figure on a cot in a dark corner. Beside him on the floor was a stretcher. He must have just delivered the patient in the rescue wagon. When Linny came closer, she saw that it was Hopping Frog.

"Doctor, can you spare a minute to look at this one?" Jared said. "I think he's bad off."

Young Doc's head jerked up. "I'll be right there," he said. He moved swiftly toward the corner cot and put his stethoscope on the patient's chest. He shook his head. "Do you know who he is?"

"A French Canadian from up north," Jared said. "He

drove stage and the school bus. The villagers called him Hopping Frog, he was always in such a hurry."

Doc beckoned to a redheaded woman in a green velveteen suit who emerged from the shadows. "Never mind trying to take his clothes off," he said. "Throw a blanket over him and give him some tea. If there's any change, let me know."

Mrs. Link spoke up. "Well, here we are come to help, Doctor. What you want we should do first?"

"I can help too," Linny said, ripping off her dripping hat and coat.

Young Doc's bright, intelligent eyes rested on Mrs. Link's solid figure as, neat in blue calico and starched white apron, she emerged from her cocoon of wrappings.

"Glad to see you two," Doc said wearily. "These patients are all in shock. The rescue wagon brought them in when their cars were blown over. Cover them warmly and improvise as many hot-water bottles as you can. Then make them some hot tea."

He ran a distraught hand through his thick hair. "I need more light," he said to Linny. "You run up to the attic and see if you can rustle up some kerosine lamps."

He turned back to the child. Linny's flesh quivered as she saw him plunge a needle into one small arm. Mrs. Link gave her a shove in the middle of her back, and she sped up the attic stairs, sorry that there had been no time to speak to Jared.

When she came back with two ancient lanterns with blackened globes, Mrs. Link was filling kettles with water. Mart was in the kitchen building a fire in the stove.

"Mart, how did you get here?" Linny questioned, relieved to see Mart's calm face.

"Sophronie is looking after the baby. Jared brought me over in the rescue wagon. I guess he will have a night of it. There are accidents everywhere, with so many bridges down."

Mrs. Link broke in. "Linny, here's a can of kerosine I found in the shed."

Linny washed the blackened globes of the lamps, filled them with kerosine, lighted them, and took them into the hospital room.

"Good girl," Doc said briefly. "Set one over in the corner for the redheaded lady and the other where my wife is."

When Linny set a lantern on a small table in the corner by Hopping Frog, the redhead was bent down over the cot. When she straightened up, Linny looked into opaque green eyes set in a thin, angular face. A sprinkling of freckles dusted her nose, and the smooth red hair was pulled tightly back from her creamy forehead. In her green suit and heavy gold bracelets she looked strangely out of place here. Linny was conscious of herself standing there like an awkward child.

"Thanks for the light," the woman said in a deep, husky voice. "I'm Laila Wells. My husband works for the Power Company. We had some car trouble . . . and then came the hurricane, so I dropped in to help out."

The stranger's wife! Linny thought in amazement. "I'm Linny Storrs from Chase Hill," she said, not mentioning that she had met Mr. Wells.

Laila was absorbed in her patient. "Doctor," she called sharply, and in three strides Doc was across the room.

"He looks bad. And he wants a cigarette," Laila murmured.

Linny peered down at the familiar face looking pasty-white against the pillow, his breath coming fast.

Doc reached under the blanket for a limp arm, felt

the pulse, and shrugged his shoulders. "Give it to him," he said, and went back to the other patients.

Linny watched Laila take out a gold cigarette case from her handbag, light a cigarette, and put it between Hopping Frog's lips. He tried to puff, but his lips trembled and his eyes seemed to be bursting from his head. A gurgling rattle came from his throat.

Laila grabbed the cigarette. "Linny," she said sharply, "you run out and throw this in the stove."

In the kitchen Mrs. Link and Mart were pouring hot water into glass jars. Linny lifted the stove lid and tossed in the cigarette. Morning and evening, Hopping Frog had always had a cigarette dangling from his mouth.

When she went back into the hospital room, Doc was bent over the bed, his ear laid against Hopping Frog's chest. He straightened up and pulled up the blanket over the still face.

"We better get him out of here. We need the room," Doc said, looking at Laila. "Think you could help me get him upstairs?"

"I can help Mrs. Wells," Linny burst out. Her throat felt dry. Her legs had a queer weakness in them. I'm not going to be chicken, she told herself sternly.

Doc eyed her doubtfully. "Every minute counts. Those that still have a chance need me."

"I'm a country girl, and I'm strong as an ox," Linny said stoutly. It was lucky Doc couldn't see inside her quivering stomach.

Doc's hand brushed her shoulder. "Okay," he said, and he was gone.

You wouldn't think a dead man would be so heavy, Linny thought as she backed up the stairs holding. Hopping Frog's shoulders while Laila held his feet. A curious calm possessed her. They struggled into the front bedroom and laid Hopping Frog down on the bed. Laila dropped his feet as if they were hotcakes. The wind had blown open the blinds and shattered the window glass. Rain was pouring in on the gloor.

"We better do something about that window," Laila said. "The rain will leak through the floor right onto the hospital beds downstairs."

"I saw some wire in the attic," Linny said. "I'll get it."

When she came running back, rain was sweeping in on Laila's green suit as she held on to the blinds she had managed to swing shut. Linny wired the blinds together. Then she snatched up a scatter rug from the floor and tucked it securely over the top of the blinds.

"There, I guess it's tight now," she said.

Laila brushed off her wet, soiled hands. She looked at the still shape on the bed. "Do you know if he has any family?"

Linny shook her head. "He lived alone in a rooming house. He was the stage driver. We saw the stage lying in the road when we came down. The hurricane must have blown it over on top of him."

Laila shivered. "Come on, Linny," she said gently and put her hand on Linny's elbow. Her face was pale, but the wide, generous mouth was steady. "We'd better see what else we can do to help, downstairs."

Meanwhile, the roar outside seemed to have gathered force. The little house shook as the wind beat against it like a battering ram. A hundred-mile gale could blow over a man easy as a straw, Linny thought. Grandpa's old bones were light and brittle as a hollow tree. As for Jan . . . She had a sudden vision of Jan crawling along the levee with a sandbag and the wind sweeping him off as if he were a fly.

Resolutely Linny put such thoughts out of her mind. She helped Laila shake out sheets and make beds, pull off socks and shoes, and helped ease bandaged patients into the cots.

Mart showed Linny how to put on bandages. "You are as skilled as a nurse," Mrs. Adams said to Mart. "Where did you learn to bandage like that?"

"My ma taught me when we lived up on Freezin' Hole," Mart said. "The loggers were always having accidents, and a doctor was a long way off."

Under Mart's skilled direction Linny learned quickly. When at last there was a lull she said, "Mart, do you suppose Grandma is all right?"

Mart kept right on rolling bandages. "Don't you worry about your grandma, Linny. It would take more than a hurricane to blow her away."

When the bandages were finished, Mart pulled on her raincoat. "You folks are getting caught up here. I better go across the road to the vestry. They'll be needing an extra hand there to cook for the men at the dam."

After Mart left, new patients staggered in, many of them with cuts on their faces and arms. They brought fresh reports of houses unroofed, barns whipped from their foundations, chicken houses scattered. Down country a woman and three children crouching in the upper story of their house had been swept into the river and had not been seen since. Rumors grew like snowballs. Beyond the black wall of the unknown no one was sure of anything.

Linny listened in numb silence. If the roof caved in, Grandma, being so lame, probably couldn't move fast enough to get out of the way. If she was hurt, if she called out, there'd be no one to hear her but the woodchucks under the house.

"Linny," Mrs. Link scolded, "you can bank on it that the minute trouble sets in, talk will grow taller than corn in August. Mercy's sakes, we haven't got a clean teacup. Now you wash up them dishes and make a fresh pot of tea."

Building up the fire with kindling to make it burn hotter, Linny shut her ears to the rumors. She got the teakettle going and hailed Mrs. Link the next time she came in the kitchen.

"You sit down and rest a minute. The water is hot, and I'll make you a cup of tea," Linny said.

Mrs. Link dropped into a kitchen chair and wiped her hot face on her limp apron. "I declare, I am tuckered," she said.

Linny felt calmer now. She looked in the cupboard and found a pot of jam and a package of crackers. She spread jam on some crackers for Mrs. Link, poured her a cup of tea. "Nothing like tea to put new life into a body," Mrs. Link said. "I better get back to work now. I'll send in the redhead for a little snack."

When Laila came out she sank into the chair vacated by Mrs. Link and stretched out her long legs wearily. "I feel like a doll that's lost its sawdust. The doctor's wife is still going. I don't see how she stands it."

Her hair lay in wisps around her neck, and her face was shiny with perspiration so that the freckles stood out sharp and clear. The green velveteen suit was a soaked and spotted ruin. But she was no longer a stranger, not after they had worked together like that, cleaning up injuries, washing away dirt and blood.

"Have a cup of tea and you'll feel better," Linny said.

She watched Laila eat crackers and jam hungrily and gulp down two cups of tea.

"Laila," she said, surprised at the ease with which the name came out, "do you think everything's all right at the dam?"

Laila pushed away her cup. She picked up her

handbag and took out a gold compact. After powdering her nose she gave a swift red dab at her lips. "No use worrying, Linny," she said.

Linny watched Laila scrub at the spots on her suit with a piece of Kleenex. She opened up her cigarette case, but it was empty.

"I'll run in and get you a cigarette from Doc," Linny said.

"No, wait!" Laila lifted her head and listened. "Do you hear what I hear?"

Linny listened too. Suddenly she realized there was no roar of wind. It was as quiet as a graveyard. The front door stood wide open, and Mrs. Link, Doc, and Mrs. Adams stood on the lawn. Mrs. Link's head was tilted back to look up at the dark sky. Her arms were folded calmly across her stomach.

Linny dashed out of the kitchen and stopped short beside Mrs. Link. "Linny, the hurricane is done and gone," she said.

"I wonder how things are going down at the dam?" Linny said in a small voice. She tried to peer into the dark. How much of the road was still passable one could only guess.

Across the road the vestry door stood open. Lamplight streamed out, and the fragrant smell of baked beans and coffee drifted over to them.

Mrs. Link's cheery voice broke the silence. "The village women are cooking for the menfolks at the dam," she said. "Doc, you and the missus better run over and get a bite."

Doc rubbed a weary hand across his tired eyes. His wife stood at his elbow, her starched uniform crumpled and bloodstained.

"We could do with a cup of coffee," Doc said.

Mrs. Link pointed up the hill, where lantern lights

twinkled on the road. Women by twos and threes with market baskets over their arms were heading for the church, bringing pies and beans.

"If any injured come up from the dam, we'll call you," Mrs. Link said. "You folks better get some food and rest. Likely you'll have a night of it." She nodded at Laila. "And you too," she said in a kindly voice.

Mrs. Link saw Linny looking up at the dark hill road. "Linny, you can't get up that road. You better wait here with us until your grandpa gits back."

Linny shook her head. "No, I've got to get home now and see how Grandma made out."

She felt Doc's hand on her shoulder. "How old are you?" he asked abruptly.

"Seventeen."

"If you ever think of wanting to train for a nurse, let me know. I'll give you a reference."

He took his wife by one arm and Laila by the other and together they went across the road toward the smell of coffee and beans.

Mrs. Link chuckled. "He means you done real good, Linny. Best take one of them lanterns with you if you're really set on getting on up the hill now."

It was slow going up the hill. With the lantern clutched tight in her hand, Linny scrambled over the wet limbs and tree trunks that were stretched across the road. If the hurricane could wipe out the road like this, she thought, her throat tightening, what must it have done to the house? She urged her tired legs on faster. The lantern flickered, and she gave it a little shake, hoping fervently there was enough kerosine to last until she got home. It was such a tiny light, but it was a light and it held back the dark.

How many thousands of years had men had lights? she wondered. Perhaps long ago those early dwellers who had carved the primitive pictures on the rocks at Bellows Falls had climbed Vermont hills bearing pitch-pine torches. Perhaps they, too, had known the big winds and run screaming in terror to get out of the way. She stopped to let her breath ease up in her. It was comforting to think of others long ago who had faced such a storm. She stumbled against a branch, caught herself, and plunged on, feeling somehow not alone in the dark.

When she reached the yard she held the lantern high in her hand, almost afraid to look. Her heart leaped. There was the house, and the barn too. Grandma had got the blinds closed all right. Only the chicken houses were gone. And the raspberries. The wind had made a clean sweep. There wasn't a cane left. She lifted the lantern higher and let out a cry. Was that a tree fallen on the ell part of the house? "Grandma!" she shrieked, and hurried across the yard and through the kitchen door.

The kitchen was a litter of plaster, torn wallpaper, shattered glass, and fallen boards. A tangle of branches had come right through the ceiling. But at the living-room table in the light of a kerosine lamp Grandma sat solid as rock, her thick fingers dealing cards.

"Grandma, are you all right?" Linny gasped.

Grandma raised her head. "So you're home," she muttered. "Where's Newt?"

"Down at the dam with every man in town." A sudden weakness seized Linny's knees as she eyed the hole in the roof. By what miracle had Grandma escaped?

"I thought likely when I heard the church bell. Didja lose the hoss?"

"Fan's safe in the Links' barn." Her blood felt as if it had turned to water, and a weak feeling gripped her stomach.

Grandma grunted and pushed her heavy body to her feet. "Set now. There's hot coffee, johnnycake, and bacon. Look in the warming oven."

Linny stumbled toward the table, her legs caving in under her, and sank into a chair. Grandma's strong hand clutched her elbow in a firm grip. "Steady, young'un. Come now, eat up your victuals." She poured a cup of coffee and held it to Linny's lips. Linny drank and struggled to push back the faintness. She could hear the cows bawling their heads off in the barn."The Jerseys are safe," she said in a thankful whisper. "I ought to get out there and milk them."

"I guess they can wait until you get your stomach full." Grandma sank down in her rocker and reached into her pocket for some spruce gum.

The coffee warmed Linny's stomach, and her head cleared. She eyed the tangle of branches in the kitchen and shuddered. "Grandma, how'd you ever get out of the way?"

"I jest set," she muttered. "I knew if 'twas comin' my way it 'ud come."

She chewed her gum lustily, her firm jaw jutting out. "What's the news down to the village?" she asked. "Anybody hurt? I want to know what's goin' on in this town!"

After giving Grandma the news Linny milked the cows the best she could. She set down the full milk pail in the kitchen for Grandma to take care of and staggered to the couch in the corner by Grandma's geraniums. Collapsing face downward on the couch, she was dimly conscious of Grandma pulling off her muddy boots and throwing the buffalo robe over her. Her eyelids seemed pinned down by weights, but in the darkness horrible visions haunted her. It was the morning Sven Peterson had gone into the tunnel and they had brought him out on a stretcher. No, it wasn't Sven on the stretcher, it was Jan. She gave a little moan and stirred restlessly. Mingling with her dream came the squeak of Grandma's rockers and her lusty old voice lifted up in song.

> I'm living on the mountain
> Underneath a cloudless sky,
> I'm drinking at a fountain
> That never shall run dry,
> Oh yes! I'm feasting on the manna
> From a bountiful supply
> For I am dwelling in Beu-lah Land!

Linny's body went limp and she slept.

18.

ALL NIGHT with furious haste the men shoveled soggy sand into burlap bags. They threw the bags onto a truck, and another crew unloaded them at the dam three quarters of a mile away. The arms and stomach muscles of the greenhorns ached. Their hands were blistered by the wet handles of the shovels, and their wet clothes stuck to them with a clammy chill.

Hour after hour the men toiled on, shouting every time the truck came back for a fresh load, "How's it going down to the dam?"

Grandpa's shovel slowed down. Old Link straightened up stiffly and laid a hand on the middle of his stiff back. "Ain't as young as we used to be, eh, Newt?" he said.

Old Mose, driving the truck back and forth, his words searing the air when he had to stop and pull fallen trees off the road, always had the same hoarse cry, "Need more sandbags. Keep 'em comin', fellers."

They hardly noticed when the rain stopped. But when the wind changed and they could hear the angry roar of floodwaters, panic drove their shovels faster. As dawn lightened the sky they grew silent, wasting no strength on words. Now and then they leaned on their shovels in exhaustion and peered through the grayness for the lights of the truck and old Mose bringing news from the dam.

"They got sandbags piled up near three feet on the levee," old Mose yelled as he backed up the truck. He jumped down from the driver's seat and climbed into the back of the truck. "Come on, heave 'em up and I'll catch," he shouted. His mighty arms reached out, grabbed the sandbags, and tossed them on the floor of the truck as if they were chicken feed.

Grandpa, stiff and sore, leaned down to lift up a bag. As he straightened up under the heavy load, black spots swam before his eyes and his legs crumpled under him like those of a worn-out old horse. "Look out there," someone hollered, but too late. Grandpa stumbled, fell headlong, and lay still.

On Chase Hill pictures of the dam floated through Linny's mind as she slept. Floating on a beam of light, she swam up out of sleep toward the dim light that filtered through the closed blinds. A loud bang jerked her awake, and she lay tense and listening. But it was only the oven door, she realized. Last night she had collapsed on the couch in the corner by Grandma's geraniums and had been only dimly conscious of her surroundings. A plaintive bawl sounded from the barn. The cows! They had to be milked! She pushed back the buffalo robe and jumped out of bed.

Her rumpled clothes felt sticky from having been slept in. Limping toward the kitchen, her legs stiff and achy, she stared through the window at the sun-flooded yard, now empty of chickens and chicken house. The sun . . . the sun was out!

Standing by the kitchen stove in the midst of the litter, fresh as a daisy in a clean calico dress, Grandma forked golden doughnuts from a pot of bubbling grease.

Linny's eyes widened as they lighted on mountainous loaves of brown-crusted bread. Spread out over the kitchen table were apple, squash, and mince pies.

"Grandma, you've been cooking all night!"

"Your boots is under the stove, or what's left of 'em," Grandma said. She laid down her fork and broke two eggs on the iron griddle, unmindful of the branches thrusting down through the hole over her head.

Linny pulled out her boots, stiff, mud-caked, and scarred from yesterday's battle.

Grandma grinned. "Soon's you get your strength you can pile them victuals in a market basket and tote 'em down to the church. I reckon the menfolks comin' up from the dam will be hungry enough to eat a hoss."

Linny had a sudden vision of Jan stuffing himself with a whole blueberry pie in two minutes flat in a pie-eating contest at the county fair. How were things going with Jan and Grandpa? The dam *must* have held, or surely they would have heard by now, she thought.

She scrubbed her hands and face in ice-cold spring water, combed her hair, and sat down at the table. Grandma heaped her plate with eggs, bacon, fried potatoes, and a big slice from one of the hot apple pies.

"You're doing a man's work now, Linny, so don't be finicky."

Linny had just finished the last bite of pie when a quick rap sounded on the kitchen door. Before she could answer, the door was pushed open and a tired voice called, "Linny."

She sprang to her feet. "Jan!" she cried, and a wave of gratitude rushed over her. He was alive, he was here! She stumbled toward him. His hair, his clothes and shoes were caked with mud, and his grimy face was drawn with fatigue.

She clutched his arm. He must have come straight from the dam. He wouldn't be here now in his muddy clothes without any sleep . . . unless . . .

"Jan, tell me . . . the dam . . ."

He gave her a hollow grin. "The dam's okay. We piled up three feet of sandbags on the levee, and that held her. It was stiff going there for a while."

She clung to his arm, quivering like a leaf. "Oh Jan, you're safe . . . and the folks down country are safe, but . . ."

Jan interrupted her. "Smells like hot apple pie," he said.

"Jan," Linny said, holding her breath, "where's Grandpa?"

"Now take it easy." He patted her hand. "We'll get to that."

Grandma bulked in the doorway. "Young man," she thundered, "speak up. I want to know what's goin' on!"

He shifted his weight from one foot to the other. "Well," he said, looking down at his muddy boots, his brow wrinkled, "well . . . er . . . the fact is . . . while he was loading up . . ."

"How bad is he hurt?" Grandma snapped.

"I don't know," Jan blurted out. "He collapsed while they were loading up, and Mose Shawn brought him to the hospital pretty soon after daybreak. Young Doc is looking after him. That's all I know."

Linny's face paled. "I'll go down right away." She hesitated and bit her trembling lips. Though life came and went, cows had to be milked. "I've got to milk first," she said.

"I'll tend to your chores. You go along," Jan said.

No sleep, no food—with half an eye you could see he was dead on his feet, Linny thought.

"You get your belly full first, Jan," Grandma said, pouring hot water from the teakettle into a basin in the sink. "Have yourself a scrub."

He plunged into the water. "Gosh, this hot water feels good," he said.

Grandma started packing the pies and bread into a market basket. Linny hurriedly changed her clothes and pulled on her mud-caked boots. Then she started off. As she scrambled over the tree trunks, trying to keep her basket steady, she thought fiercely, Grandpa's too old. I ought never to have let him go down to the dam.

That dam! It had brought nothing but trouble.

By the time she reached the foot of Chase Hill, her forehead damp, her legs stiff and sore, she was breathing hard, but cutting through her worry came the thought that other folks had suffered too. By daylight she could see that it was worse than she had dreamed. Were there more than a handful of trees left in all Vermont?

She could hardly bear to look at the giant maples lying with their roots upended in the air. No sugar crop next spring. And no apple crop either if the orchards were wiped out. With the maples and spruces gone, there would be no forests left. The farmers would be shorn of the timber that they relied on as money in the bank. The mutilated fields lay wounded under the golden sun. How could Vermont ever survive this kind of disaster?

When she reached the springhouse she came on a crew swinging axes and hollering at their horses as they snaked big limbs off the road.

"Hi, Linny," called old Mose Shawn. "You on the way to see your grandpa?"

He sunk his ax into a tree limb, straightened up, and

pushed his felt cap on the back of his head as if he had all the time in the world.

"Mr. Shawn," she said, her voice tremulous with anxiety, "do you know how Grandpa is?"

He scratched his grizzled head and gave her an impish grin. "Linny, ain't nothin' goin' to git any better worryin' about it. Your gramp's got plenty of gumption."

Linny let out a shaky breath. "Is it like this all over Vermont?"

He shook his head. "I dunno. Likely be a week before we find out. All roads is blocked, wires down, and power off."

"But what will folks do?" She felt as if her world had collapsed.

Old Mose reached for his ax and snorted. "Why, they'll do the same as they've always done in Vermont. They'll keep a-goin'."

She looked at his weathered face, which bore few marks of yesterday's struggle, and then at his big shoulders, his strong, sturdy legs. Working around the clock for folks in trouble, he'd had no sleep or rest.

"Lend me your jackknife," she said, "and I'll cut you a quarter of an apple pie. It's still hot."

Then she headed for the village, her pace quickening. Talking to old Mose had steadied her. When she reached the vestry she carried in her load of pies and saw a line of grimy men gathered around the long tables hungrily eating baked beans, sandwiches, and coffee. Mrs. Link took the pies from Linny's basket and began cutting generous slices.

"Tell your grandma we're obliged," she said. "We've got a parcel of hungry men to feed. You on the way to see your grandpa?"

Linny nodded. "Mrs. Link, did you hear how badly he's hurt?"

She shook her head. "Young Doc hasn't been over here since last night. I reckon he's too busy."

Linny picked up her basket and made for the door. Before she could reach it, she was stopped by the stranger. His sodden clothes looked as if they were ruined for good. There was a streak of dirt along one cheek, and his grimy face was lined with fatigue. "I saw you come in," he said. "I wanted to ask about your grandfather."

"I don't know. I'm on the way to the hospital now," she said, surprised at his concern.

"Don't let me keep you," he said warmly, patting her shoulder. "Let's hope for the best. Tell your grandmother I asked about him. I hear she's a remarkable woman."

Linny excused herself and fled, her head a jumble of emotions. He had almost seemed human! And he hadn't said a word about the Power Company. Maybe, after all, it was going to turn out the way it did for the Brick House, and the Power Company wouldn't need to come up on Chase Hill.

Feeling calmer and ready to deal with what lay ahead, she pushed open the door of the hospital. The long front room was filled with patients, and Mrs. Adams, in a fresh uniform, was still busy. As soon as she saw Linny she set down the pitcher of water she was carrying. "You've come to see your grandfather, I expect, Linny. He's right over here."

In the corner where Hopping Frog had lain yesterday, Grandpa was now stretched out, still and unmoving. Linny crept close, pushed up a chair, and sat down quietly. His eyes were closed, his features sharp and clear, his long white beard reached to his chest. How beautiful he is, she thought with a lump in her throat.

She looked up questioningly into the tired face of Young Doc. He picked up Grandpa's wrist and felt his pulse. "We gave him a needle around five o'clock, and he's been sleeping ever since. He's worn out," he said.

"Is he badly hurt?" Linny breathed.

Young Doc looked grave. "He has a strong constitution. It looks as if he fractured his right leg. I've put on a temporary splint, but we need to get him over to the Bennington Hospital, where they'll take X rays and make him a proper cast. Jared and his helper have gone home to catch a bit of rest. Soon as they get back they'll take him to Bennington. They've had a busy night."

"I know," Linny said. "Cousin Jared is chief of the volunteers, and sometimes when he's called out in the night he goes to work the next day with hardly any sleep."

"They are well trained," Doc said. "I'm sure they will take good care of your grandfather, and it won't cost you a cent."

Linny gripped the edge of her chair. A broken leg! That would mean hospital care, doctors' bills, medicines, and other expenses. The chickens were gone, and so were the raspberry bushes, the sugar maples. The roof was wrecked. Never mind, she thought fiercely, if only he pulls through, we'll get along somehow.

"When he wakes up, please tell him I was here," Linny said to Mrs. Adams. "I've got to get back up the hill and let Grandma know how he is. She's worrying."

As she struggled back up the tree-blocked road she met the crew headed by old Mose Shawn again and saw they were digging out Chase Hill.

"We'll have your road clear, come tomorrow," old Mose shouted, not stopping in his work.

"Thank you," she shouted back, her throat thick with

gratitude. Taking new heart, she clambered on up Chase Hill.

Her knees were buckling under her when she reached the top of the hill. In the house Grandma sat rocking in her rocker as if she were a forty-niner headed for the gold fields. As soon as Linny came through the doorway the rocking stopped and she snapped out, "How's Newt?"

No use trying to keep it from her. Grandma had to know. "Young Doc says he has a broken leg. He's sending him over to the Bennington Hospital in the community rescue wagon," she said. "Jared was up all night, and he's gone home to get some rest."

Grandma drew a deep breath and began rocking again. "He's strong as an ox. I reckon he'll come through it all right. Could be worse."

"Grandma, you didn't get any sleep last night. Why don't you lie down now and rest a bit?" Linny urged.

"No, my head gits to buzzin' around if I lie down. I'd rather be up and doing. Soon's the telephone line gits fixed I'll call Jared. Likely he'll git the tree off the roof for us."

"Jan said he would tell Jared," Linny said.

The very next day Jared showed up, bringing his chain saw with him. He and Jan got the tree off and laid a temporary patch on the roof.

Linny swept up the leaves and litter on the kitchen floor, gratefully listening to the hum of Jared's chain saw. How could they ever repay him for all his work? And Jan too.

Each night and morning Jan showed up to do the chores. One night, as Linny watched him with his head pressed against the flanks of a Jersey while he milked, she thought of the many times she had reproached him for going to work at the Power Company. She dropped down on a wooden sawhorse.

"Jan, I'm sorry," she said. "I know I'm unreasonable about the Power Company. I just can't help it."

Jan swung up from the milking stool and picked up the pail frothing with milk. "You've always been against the Power Company, Linny. It's like trying to swim upstream. You can't stop things from changing. Nobody can, any more than you could have stopped the hurricane. Sadawga Springs is changing . . . yes . . . but you have to go with it. That's the way life is."

Seeing Jan stand there, so strong and steady on his feet, made her wish she could feel as he did. She took the milk pail from his hand. "You stay and have supper with us, Jan, before you go back down the hill. Grandma has made some gingerbread especially for you."

In a few days the going was easier, with Chase Hill road open. By the end of the week most roads were cleared and wires restrung. Telephones were working again, and the stage operated by old Mose Shawn and his blacks was on the road until the town could buy a new bus.

Grandma was on the telephone, one great hand clamped over the mouthpiece as she listened in to tales from down country. Help poured in from the Red Cross. The homeless were fed and sheltered and set their faces toward the future. At last rumor was discarded for the truth. The hurricane had swept through seven states, and more than seven hundred lives had been lost.

"Jumpin' Jehoshaphat, did you ever hear of such goin's on?" Grandpa exclaimed in excitement.

Linny, scratching figures on a pad at the dining-room table, paid little attention to Grandma. If she could scrape together some old boards, maybe she could build a chicken house herself. With Jan's help she might snake out some of the hurricane logs in the woods and sell them. That would pay for a new roof over the kitchen before winter.

Linny went on with her figuring. They had plenty of hay, more than they needed. Some folks would be short of hay and glad to buy. But they would have to pay something at the Bennington Hospital. Grandpa would have apoplexy if the Red Cross offered him aid.

Grandma hung up the receiver and sat down in her chair. She gave a great sigh. "Linny, I dunno as it's any use for you to figger. Your grandpa's bad off. 'Twill be a long time before he's able to work again, if ever. I look to see Nat and Gloria any day now, and they'll be wantin' to lug us all off down country. Looks like this time we're done beat."

Linny rose from the table. "Why, Grandma, fancy you talking so! Grandpa's holding his own, isn't he? I've got health and strength . . . and there's the land. . . ."

But her heart was not as brave as her words. Slowly she trudged down the cleared hill to the store, trying to get up the courage to ask Hal Eames to trust her for a pair of stout work shoes. They needed groceries too.

Hal Eames let her have the shoes and the groceries and, to her astonishment, said, "You don't need to be in any hurry to pay."

She went over to the Link house to thank Mr. Link and then ride old Fan home bareback now the road was clear. Mr. Link seemed to be in no hurry to let her go.

"How's your grandpa?" he asked Linny.

"He's holding his own," she said, lifting the reins and trying to hold Fan still.

"Kit ain't takin' on none," he said, making a flat

statement that expected no answer. He seemed to be in no hurry, and Linny resigned herself to listen.

There was a faraway look in his eyes. He ran a rough hand over his sharp, unshaven chin. "Tell you what," he growled, "I hear you folks are bad off. I'd be obliged if you'd ask your grandma would she accept a loan from me until you get back on your feet."

"Why, Mr. Link!" Linny said. She looked at him in surprise, and thought of how folks called him the tightest man in Sadawga Springs.

He muttered something under his breath and strode off.

When Linny reached home and told Grandma what Mr. Link had said, Grandma rocked and rocked, her eyes bright as new dollars. "I swan," she said, "think of Link offerin' to part with cold cash!"

"What will Aunt Gloria and Uncle Nat say?" Linny asked.

"We best wait and find out," Grandma said.

They didn't have long to wait, because Aunt Gloria and Uncle Nat arrived that same day, and the air was loud with glad shrieks and exclamations.

"So the old house still stands!" Uncle Nat said. "Takes more than a hurricane to blow her down, to say nothing of you, Ma." He poked her in the ribs with a sly grin.

"How'd you folks git here?" Grandma demanded.

"We hopped a ride on a cable truck," Gloria said, breathless and excited. "Why, Ma, they've sent linemen up to Vermont clear from the Middle West."

Grandma's eyes rested on Gloria's hair, which was wisping down over her face, and took in her rumpled suit. "I vum, fancy you ridin' on a truck, Gloria."

"So you lost the chicken house." Uncle Nat rubbed his hands together. "Well, I can still handle a saw and hammer. Bet I can put up the best chicken house in seven counties."

"Oh, darlings!" Gloria moaned, her gentle cheeks flushed. "When we couldn't get any news of you for almost a week, we nearly went crazy. Nat and I talked it all over on the way up, and we vowed that if you were spared to us, you would never have another worry."

"That's right," Nat beamed. "We got it all figured out. We're going to send you enough to live on, and send it regularly."

Linny stared at Grandma, thinking of Mr. Link's offer, and waited to hear what she would say.

"Land o' Goshen!" Grandma exploded, rising to the occasion. "I always knew I could count on my young'uns." Her bright eyes twinkled. "Ain't it the truth now? A Vermonter always looks after his own."

Linny knew for a certainty that wild horses wouldn't drag a word out of Grandma about Mr. Link.

"Uncle Nat, will you buy me some more raspberry bushes?" she asked. "I think we can sell some hurricane lumber, too." If they all pulled together, she knew they could make out. Happily she began stirring up dough for hot biscuits and opened up a jar of wild strawberry jam for Uncle Nat.

Gloria and Uncle Nat poked their noses into attic and cellar, made plans, argued, wrote down interminable lists of window glass, putty, chicken wire, nails. "We must get some weatherstripping too, Nat, so we can plug up some of these places that let in drafts," Gloria said.

Nat took off the coat of his good suit, put on Grandpa's worn old sweater, and headed for the chicken yard.

In her rocker by the window Grandma was reading the Boston newspapers Uncle Nat had brought. Her rockers stopped still as she read aloud tales of heroism, of telephone girls sticking to their posts through fire and flood, of linemen heroically battling the elements, risking their lives to string wires. Plain Joe Smith was the hero of the hour.

"Glory hallelujah!" Grandma exclaimed, her rockers pitching wildly. "Don't it beat all! Let trouble smack hard enough, and fellow feelin's grow faster'n a man's beard."

Linny, busy with her baking, listened with half an ear. She opened up a jar of home-canned raspberries and made a raspberry pie. Uncle Nat, banging away in the chicken yard, was working up an appetite. And there was the milking for Uncle Nat to do. They had depended on Jan long enough. Perhaps it would be better to give up trying to keep cows. It would be months before Grandpa got his strength back, if ever.

She floured the breadboard and rolled out cookie dough for Grandpa's favorite molasses cookies, And just in time, because Jared brought Grandpa back from the hospital in the community rescue wagon.

But when Grandpa tried to make his way with crutches, he almost fell. "What you need is a wheelchair you can negotiate yourself," Gloria said.

"Young Doc will lend us a chair," Linny said, and hurried down to the hospital, and with the help of Jared and the volunteers, Grandpa got the chair the same day.

With Grandpa comfortably installed in the chair and rolling himself around, Linny wiped her hands on her apron and hastened to fix tea and cookies for everyone.

Grandpa stationed himself in front of the kitchen window, where he could watch Nat building the chicken house. "I declare, I never thought Nat was any hand with a hammer," he said in wonder.

Linny opened the oven door and poured a bit of

maple syrup over the baking beans. She'd make a dish of cole slaw and fry some bacon to go with the beans. New hope flowered in her. They were all together. In spite of the hurricane, they would make out. If only the Power Company would leave them alone!

19

LINNY CREPT QUIETLY down the front staircase so as not to waken Uncle Nat and Aunt Gloria, who were sleeping in the back bedroom below. They had sat up late last night arguing about fixing the old house up, with never a word about the Power Company.

In the living room Grandpa sat in his wheelchair fully dressed, his crutches leaning against a table.

"Why, Grandpa, you're up early," Linny said, taking a stick of wood from his hand. "Let me stoke the fire."

"Kitchen fire's gone out," Grandpa said. "Before you build it up, look in on your grandma. She's ailin'."

Linny threw the wood into the stove and hurried to the door of the bedroom. Under a mountain of bed-clothes Grandma lay stretched out still and unmoving, her eyes closed.

"Grandma," Linny said, fear springing up in her at Grandma's unnatural quietness, "are you all right?"

Grandma's eyelids fluttered open. When she spoke her voice slurred thickly and sounded weak and shaky. "I can't move my left leg, Linny. Guess you'll have to git Young Doc to come see me."

Linny laid a hand on Grandma's forehead. No fever. She straightened up the bedclothes and said, "I'll get him right away, Grandma."

Lucky that the line had been repaired, she thought, as

she twirled the handle of the phone. Young Doc was there and would come up right away.

In the kitchen Linny built up a hot fire with kindling, put on a kettle of water to heat, and measured out coffee, trying to think only of the present. As soon as breakfast was ready she'd call Uncle Nat and Aunt Gloria. If Grandma was going to be laid up, it might change their plans.

Quickly she stirred up a batch of biscuits, cooked bacon, got out eggs and some of Grandma's jelly. As soon as the coffee was hot she took a cup to Grandma, who drank it gratefully and said, "I don't want nothin' to eat."

Grandma was really sick if she couldn't eat, Linny thought nervously. She wished Young Doc would hurry.

She called Uncle Nat and Aunt Gloria, not mentioning a word about Grandma. Time enough for discussion later.

A knock sounded on the door, and she flew to open it. It was comforting to see Young Doc standing there, clean-shaven, spruce, and competent-looking. She showed him into Grandma's bedroom, then flew back to the kitchen to turn the bacon.

Uncle Nat came in rubbing his hands and smiling. "My, that bacon smells good, Linny," he said.

"Uncle Nat, there's bad news this morning," Linny said. "Grandma's ailing and Young Doc is here."

Swift alarm swept over Nat's face. "Ma's always been healthy as a horse."

Gloria appeared, pulling on a thick sweater. "What's the matter with Ma?" she demanded.

"Young Doc will tell us," Linny said. "Why don't you folks have a cup of coffee now."

While they sipped their coffee Linny went into the bedroom to see if Young Doc had finished his examination. He was just pulling up the bedclothes. From his cheery tone she guessed it was bad news.

"I don't think your grandma has got anything she won't get over . . . in time . . ." he said.

"What is it?" Linny insisted.

"She's had a minor stroke, and we better get her to a hospital right away. I can arrange to have her admitted to Bennington Hospital."

Grandma would never consent to go to a hospital, Linny thought in dismay.

Uncle Nat appeared in the doorway. "Hold on," he said. "If Ma needs to go to the hospital . . . okay. But I want her where I can keep an eye on her, and I can't be running back and forth to Bennington. Can you get her into a Boston hospital, Doctor?"

"How about the Massachusetts General?" Young Doc suggested. "She'll get the best possible care there. And I have a friend on the staff."

"Excellent," Nat said. He tweaked one of Grandma's toes under the bedspread. "They'll have you up in no time, Ma. I'll come to visit you every day," he said heartily.

Linny held her breath. Grandma never would consent to go to a hospital, to say nothing of Boston. She looked at the big mound, but Grandma never stirred.

Grandma's eyes flickered, and she seemed to be summoning all her energy to speak. "Well, git on with it. Linny, you run up to the attic and fetch me one of them suitcases. Nat and Gloria, you finish your breakfast. Dr. Adams, you call that Boston hospital. Whatcha' all waitin' for? I ain't a corpse yet."

Before going up to the attic Linny handed Grandpa

his crutches and helped him to the breakfast table. "Aunt Gloria," she said, "you give Grandpa some bacon and eggs. Breakfast is keeping warm on the stove."

While Gloria served Grandpa and Nat, Linny ran upstairs to the attic. She dusted off Grandma's old leather suitcase and brought it downstairs.

Young Doc was still there. He had put through his call to Boston and had arranged everything for Grandma.

"How can we get Ma to Boston?" Nat asked. "She can't sit up in a car."

"The community rescue wagon will take her," Doc said. "The farm boys who operate the wagon are well trained."

As Young Doc picked up his bag to go, Linny caught his arm. On impulse she blurted out, "Dr. Adams, what hospital school of nursing would you recommend?"

Dr. Adams grinned. "Are you thinking about the nursing profession, Linny? I would recommend the hospital school of nursing in Fitchburg, Massachusetts. It's an excellent hospital, and you would get valuable experience there. My wife is a graduate of that school. Why don't you come down and talk to her?"

"Thank you, Doctor, I will," Linny said gratefully. "I haven't decided yet what I'm going to do. Uncle Nat and Aunt Gloria want me to go to college. But I wish I could take care of Grandma."

"It's very important that she be kept quiet for the next ten days," he said. "If she doesn't have another stroke, she may come out of this one . . . in time."

It was impossible to think of Grandma as an invalid. Linny shut the door after Young Doc and tried to shut out dark thoughts. Grandpa couldn't be left here alone. Maybe she'd better put off going away to school and stay here to take care of Grandpa.

Grandpa had finished his breakfast and was trying to

get up on his crutches. She helped him into his wheelchair and then began clearing the table. Whatever trouble came, dishes had to be done.

Uncle Nat tramped restlessly around the kitchen. He stopped still as Grandma called from the bedroom, "Nat, I want to have a confab with you." She sounded almost like her old self.

"Wait just a minute, until I get you freshened up," Linny said, appearing in the doorway with a basin of hot water, a washcloth, and a towel. She washed Grandma's face and hands, combed her hair, and put in her pearl sidecombs. Then she puffed up her pillows and helped her into a clean nightgown.

"I declare, Linny, you'd make a good nurse," Grandma said, trying to push herself up to a sitting position.

"Now, Grandma, Young Doc said for you to be quiet, so don't talk long with Uncle Nat," Linny said.

Nat came in, his shoulders sagging. "What's on your mind, Ma?"

Grandma wasted no time beating about the bush. "The jig is up, Nat. I seen it comin' a long time back. Newt can't farm it no more, he's too old. And I'm not goin' to have you pourin' money in here like a sieve. You get hold of John Link and tell him I'm ready to sell the Newt Chase place to the Power Company."

Nat straightened up. "Ma, I'm sorry things had to end this way."

"I've known ever since Truman went it was only a matter of time. If I don't give in now, they'll get me by that thing they call eminent domain."

Nat nodded his head. "You'd only go to law to get beat. I'm glad you decided now."

"I don't know how much of an invalid I'm goin' to be, but when it comes time to leave the hospital you put me in one of them there nursing homes. You can use the money from the sale of the house to pay the hospital and all other expenses."

"Ma, I'll never let you go to a nursing home," Nat said stoutly. "Now don't you worry about a thing." He leaned down and kissed Grandma on the cheek. "You're a real trooper," he said.

"I was born on the Nate Chase place and I aimed to die on it," Grandma said, "but I guess my time ain't come yet."

The Nate Chase place would go the same as Uncle Truman's place had gone, Linny thought. She felt numb all over, as if this were happening to someone else. She mustn't think about it now . . . she must think about Grandma.

She lifted up Grandma's suitcase and set it on a chair. "Grandma, I'll pack your bag for you," she said. Her hands shook as she opened up the bureau drawers and took out Grandma's flannel nighties, her long underwear and cotton stockings. Gloria came to the door with a bar of scented soap and a bottle of toilet water. "Put these in for Ma," Gloria said. "When we get back to Boston, I'll get her a bed jacket."

"Now don't get all fussed up about me," Grandma said. "I'll be right as rain. It's Newt needs lookin' after. His bad leg won't heal fast, and his memory is forsakin' him."

"Don't you worry," Gloria said kindly. "We'll look after Pa."

At last all was ready. Gloria was sweeping up the kitchen floor. Grandpa was asleep in his chair. Linny carried out Grandma's suitcase and set it down by the door.

"Linny, bring me my cherry box," Grandma demanded.

"You're getting tired. You ought to rest now," Linny

said. But she put the box on the bed where Grandma could reach it.

"I got one more little job to do," Grandma said. She opened the box and took out Great-Grandmother Betsy Chase's brooch. She held it out to Linny.

"Here, Linny, wherever you're a-goin' you take this with you. Mind you remember who your folks was. Us Chases may not have set the world on fire, but we always stood up straight and took what come."

Linny didn't trust herself to speak. She took the brooch and pinned it to the neck of her blouse, her eyes stinging. Then she flung her arms around Grandma and held her tight. "I'll never forget as long as I live," she sobbed.

Grandma patted her on the back. "There, there," she said, "no need to go overboard. Time now, Linny, for you to stand on your own feet."

Gloria peered around the corner of the bedroom door. "The rescue wagon is here, Ma," she said.

Linny wiped away the tears, went to the closet, and got out Grandma's blue flannel robe. She helped her into the robe and pulled on Grandma's bedroom slippers.

Grandpa wheeled himself to the door of the bedroom. "What's goin' on here?" he asked anxiously.

Grandma snorted. "Now don't you git all fussed up, Newt. I'm goin' to a Boston hospital but I'll be right as rain, so don't you worry none. Nat and Gloria will let you know how I be. Take care of yourself."

Linny caught the long look that flashed between them. She patted Grandpa's shoulder as she pushed his wheelchair out of the way.

Two brawny six-footers in white jump suits appeared in the doorway. The taller one with a smile on his good-humored face said, "Ready for us?"

"It's lucky you're farm boys, 'cuz I weigh more'n a Morgan mare," Grandma said with a flash of her old fire.

"Just leave everything to us, Grandma," the shorter one said, pushing back his wavy blond hair.

In no time at all they had pushed a stretcher on wheels close to the bed, spread a gray blanket over Grandma, and placed her on the stretcher. They wheeled the stretcher out to the waiting ambulance and moved Grandma onto a bunk bed.

"Well done, boys," Grandma said in admiration. Her eyes went around the interior of the ambulance, not missing a thing. "You've got a real hospital in here," she said.

"That's right. We even delivered a baby once," the taller one said. He sat down behind the driver's wheel. His broad back was reassuring as he settled into place. Grandma heaved a sigh of relief.

The younger boy sat down on a stool beside her and took one of her hands. "Feel faint?" he asked. He got up and came back with a small basin. "Now you let me know if you feel sick to your stomach," he said.

"Vittles allus set well on my stomach," Grandma said in disdain, shoving away the basin. She waved at Grandpa, who was sitting in his wheelchair by the open door.

"Take a good look at my house, boy," she said, just before the motor sprang on, "for you'll never see it again. It's goin' down the drain of the Power Company. My ma, Betsy Chase, come to that house as a bride. . . ."

Through the open window of the ambulance drifted the sound of Grandma's rumbling voice. "Kit's off and goin' it," Grandpa chuckled. Her tongue will clack all the way to Boston."

20

ALMOST EVERYTHING was taken care of. The hogs brought only ten cents a pound. The hay in the barn they gave away. The hay wagon and rake, the farm tools, and even the Jerseys were let go at bargain prices.

The big problem was Fan. Uncle Nat said, "Who will buy an old nag like Fan? The only thing to do is to put a bullet through her head."

Linny protested, "But Fan is one of the family!"

She was thankful Jan came to the rescue. "I'll take Fan," he said.

"But Jan, you don't use horses on your farm. You've got machinery. Besides, it will cost plenty for grain to feed her," she said.

Jan grinned. "Don't worry. I'll put her out to pasture, and my brothers and sisters will make a pet of her. It's good for young ones to have something to look after."

Linny's eyes misted over. "That's good of you, Jan," she said. "Grandma and Grandpa will be so pleased."

But they wouldn't be pleased if Mr. Link got the best of Uncle Nat, Linny thought, as she picked the last of the shell beans. She kept one eye on the barn, where Mr. Link and Uncle Nat were bargaining. If Uncle Nat didn't watch out, Mr. Link would skin him, as sure as God made little apples. She yanked at the brittle bean vines. Uncle Nat would be soft as clay in Mr. Link's greedy hands. She decided to see for herself and headed for the barn.

At the west side of the barn she cupped a hand over her eyes and peered through a knothole. Mr. Link was leaning back against a beam while Uncle Nat squatted on a keg of nails. They were eyeing each other like two rattlers.

Uncle Nat's fingers played with the creases of his blue suit. "You can't trim me," he barked. "I know lumber's worth money."

Five acres of spruce alone, Linny thought. She and Grandpa had reckoned there were better than 400,000 feet in the woodlot, and spruce was needed to build ships, Grandpa had said.

"That timber ain't worth so much. All second growth," Mr. Link drawled. "No hard wood at all. All you got here is view, and that ain't worth nothin' to the Power Company."

A sudden swoop of a plane buzzing overhead drowned out the rest of Link's words. Drat that plane! Linny thought. It vanished into the blue, and she struggled to hear through the knothole again.

Uncle Nat's forehead was wrinkled in uncertainty. He pulled out his watch and looked at it.

"Well, there's my proposition. Take it or leave it," Mr. Link said. He was licking his lips like a cat over a mouse.

Linny strode into the barn. "Uncle Nat, the shipyards are looking for spruce to build ships with, and they pay from five to six dollars a thousand on the stump. You raise Mr. Link a thousand and don't take a penny less."

Mr. Link burst into a loud guffaw. He eyed Linny with admiration. She turned on her heel and fled.

"Hey, Linny," she heard him call after her, but she marched steadily toward the house.

The house was dank with chill. Aunt Gloria had forgotten to put wood in the stove, and the fire was out. Grandpa, sniffling with a cold, sat huddled up in Grandma's rocker, a red plaid blanket over his knees. She started to build up the fire.

"That you, Linny?" he said in a hoarse voice. "Did you see anyone come up the road a while back? My eyesight's gettin' poor. I thought I see old Link. If it was him he ain't here for no good."

His dim blue eyes looked at her, waiting for an answer.

"You're seeing things, Grandpa," she said, tucking the blanket firmly around him. "I've put some kindling on, and it will be warm here in a minute."

He began to rock a little. "It's awful quiet around here with your grandma gone," he complained. "I vum, I wish somebody would make some noise."

"You ought to have a radio, Grandpa. It would be company," she said.

His eyes brightened. "That's so," he sighed. "But I reckon it would cost a pretty penny."

"Did you see the plane go over, Grandpa?" she said, trying to distract him.

He pressed his white head to the pane again. "Say, Linny, you sure you didn't see old Link?"

She hurried into the front hall before he could ask her again.

Slowly she climbed the stairs and turned away from the empty bedroom where she had slept since she was a child. Great-Grandmother Betsy Chase's four-poster bed and walnut dresser had been sold. But Betsy's log-cabin quilt that Mart had given her was packed safely away in her trunk. Where the trunk was going she'd have to decide soon. Time was getting short.

There were jobs down country in factories, but she'd

be no hand around machinery. People, now, were another matter. Ads in newspapers called for trained nurses. But if she decided to enroll as a student nurse, Aunt Gloria would make a dreadful fuss. "You'd better come down to Boston with us," Aunt Gloria had said. "It's not too late to go to art school and make something of your talent."

Linny sighed as she climbed the attic stairs. She picked her way across the dusty attic floor, stepping over piles of newspapers, schoolbooks, and empty bottles.

"Is that you, dear?" Gloria's voice came muffled from the depths of an old trunk. She straightened up her slim back, her face red and hot, streaks of dust straddling her nose.

"I've finished the beans," Linny said. Surveying the confusion, she thought how every spring Grandma had said she was going to clean out the attic. "Can I help up here?"

"Throw this out the attic window, will you, dear? It's all rotted." Aunt Gloria's fingertips held at arm's length a moth-eaten blue army coat with brass buttons.

Linny's hands clenched together. "But, Aunt Gloria, you're not going to throw away the first Nathan Chase's Revolutionary Army coat!"

Gloria sighed. "Linny, you're as bad as your grand-parents. I don't think they ever threw away so much as a piece of string."

"But, Aunt Gloria . . ."

Gloria pushed back her hair with a distracted hand and looked around the attic as if it were a mountain on her shoulders. "Darling, who could take all this stuff? Nat wouldn't give it house room."

"Maybe Uncle Nat won't like having Grandpa either," Linny flared up.

"Now, Linny, I've got a woman in mind," Gloria said. "She's conscientious and efficient, and she'll look after your grandpa well."

But there was a worried frown between Linny's eyes. She stepped over a cracked chamber pot, picked up the old blue coat, and moved toward the window. As she leaned out to drop the coat on the pile below, she saw Uncle Nat and Mr. Link come out of the barn. They stood in the road still talking.

Gloria bent over her shoulder and saw the men. She wiped her hands over and over on her apron. "I guess we better go down," she said.

Linny let the coat drop to the ground. In silence they made their way down the steep attic stairs. Linny opened the door and went out into the yard, where stuff thrown out the attic window was strewn all around. On top of a pile of moth-eaten blankets lay an old photograph in a broken wire frame. Linny bent down and picked it up. A boy in tight knee pants sat on the edge of a sofa, his face set in a forced smile. She could hear Grandma chuckle. "We took Nat over to Brattleboro to git that picture took. When we got home, afore I could get that suit off Nat, he had to go and git mixed up with a skunk. Even if 'twas his only good suit we had to bury his clothes in the pasture from the skin out."

Uncle Nat rounded the corner of the house. He stopped and stood looking at Link's retreating back.

Gloria's eyes followed Nat's. "How did you make out, Nat?" she asked, her hands picking at her crumpled apron.

Without answering, Nat scowled down at the pile of trash. His eye lighted on the picture in Linny's hand, and he smiled.

"That was the day you got mixed up with a skunk, Uncle Nat," Linny reminded him.

He let out a haw. "Do I remember! I thought I was going to make a pet out of a skunk!"

"Nat, I asked how you made out?" Gloria said sharply.

He flipped out his handkerchief and wiped his sweating forehead. "Well, I didn't get trimmed as badly as I might have if Linny hadn't butted in. I raised him a thousand, Linny, like you said."

He stuck his hands in his pockets. His narrow shoulders sagged, and a forlorn look crept over his face.

"There was nothing else to do," Gloria said in a shaky voice.

"Nope." Nat straightened up, and his foot landed a good kick on the pile of trash. "I'll get a man to cart this stuff to the dump. Now let's clear out of here as fast as we can."

Gloria nodded as she disappeared inside the house. Linny lingered by the pile, trying to get used to the reality that the house and almost everything they had owned were now actually gone.

Uncle Nat shifted from foot to foot. "Say, Linny . . . I . . . er . . . that is, I suppose you are thinking about going to college, but I want you to know that you are welcome to make your home with us as long as you like, whatever you do. Pa and Ma will be there, and we'll try to make things homelike."

"Thanks, Uncle Nat," she said gently. "I haven't decided yet what I'm going to do."

In the kitchen she found Gloria packing dishes in a barrel: the white china setting hen, the blue willow plates, the hobnail glasses. She picked up a blue glass hat. "Sandwich," Gloria said. "I suppose we might sell some of this glass to an antique shop."

"But, Aunt Gloria, that's Grandpa's toothpick holder!" Linny protested.

Gloria's hands dropped helplessly to her side. "Linny,

dear, why don't you run down to the store. You can get the mail and your grandma's *Deerfield Valley Times.* Cancel the subscription. Make out one of those change-of-address cards, too."

"I will, Aunt Gloria," she said, and turned away.

She saw Grandpa's white head pressed to the pane. "I thought I see old Link," he muttered.

Linny fled.

When she reached the springhouse she stopped and pumped herself a drink of iron water. As she hung the cup back on the nail she saw Mr. Butterfield's gaunt frame perched on a ladder. He was banging away with a hammer. She hurried across the road and stopped at the foot of the ladder. He grinned down at her. "Howdy, Linny."

"Mr. Butterfield, what are you up to, up there on that ladder?" she said, smiling up at him.

"Hal Eames has cleared out." He squinted down at her, and one eyelid flicked her a wink.

"Why, Mr. Butterfield, you don't mean you bought the store back?" Linny gasped.

He swung his hammer quick as a young man, his hat pushed to the back of his head. "Been a Butterfield in this here store ever since the day when every customer got a free drink of rum with his goods," he said cheerily. "Guess the chain was glad enough to git rid of the store, what with the village shrinkin' every day."

He pried up the chain-store sign, let it drop to the ground with a clatter, and brushed off his hands. "Got anything you want to trade, Linny?"

"Ten pounds of baking beans."

"I'll take 'em," he said promptly. "Pick out what you want to trade for."

She thought a minute. "Mr. Butterfield, have you any of those little radios that Mr. Eames had?"

He shook his head. "Nope, I ain't. Scarcer 'n hen's teeth. Dunno where you could pick one up."

"I want one for Grandpa," she said. "He says he wants to hear a little noise."

Cautiously Mr. Butterfield backed down the ladder. He scratched his thin hair. "Tell you what. That Jew feller up to the Brick House, he's sellin' out like you folks. Maybe he has a little radio for sale."

"Why, Cousin Joe's old phonograph might still be up in the attic. I bet his nephew wouldn't even have bothered to pick it up," Linny said in excitement.

"That's so, it might," agreed Mr. Butterfield. He opened the store door for Linny.

The old familiar tinkle sounded as Linny stepped in. She smiled as she twirled the dial of their mailbox and took out Grandma's paper. After canceling the paper and making out a change-of-address card, she waved good-bye to Mr. Butterfield and started off down the road toward the Brick House.

As she walked along the wood road she saw that the grass in the mowing had not been cut and that the ground was thick with rotting apples. A lonely place, she thought. Hardly a soul came up this road in six months. She couldn't imagine why a musician by the name of Goldstein should want to leave New York and come up here to live in these backwoods.

She turned into the yard of the Brick House. The front door stood open. At the sound of her footsteps a short, dark-jowled man wearing glasses came to the door and glowered at her. He waited for her to speak.

Linny knew that with him she couldn't make small talk the way Cousin Joe and Grandpa used to do before getting down to business. She'd have to state her errand quickly to this man.

"I heard in the store that you are selling out," she began tentatively.

He scowled down at her from beneath dark brows. "Most everything's gone. What are you looking for?"

"A radio," she said hopefully.

"The radio is not for sale," he said, looking as if he had swallowed a chunk of alum.

"Oh . . ." She hesitated. "Well, I was wondering if you might still have an old Edison phonograph that came with the house."

He glared at her. "I wouldn't sell that old-timer for love or money," he growled.

"Good day, Mr. Goldstein," she said, and turned on her heel.

"Hold on," he called after her. "Come in and we'll talk it over."

In the house Linny saw that the parlor was in wild disorder, half empty of furniture. She noticed a small radio standing on a side table. A handsome Colonial mirror still hung over the fireplace. She laid a reverent hand on a satin-smooth maple chair. "I remember those chairs from my childhood," she said.

"Those Fiddlebacks brought a good price," he said gloomily. He gave a deep sigh. "Never get such good stuff together again."

His face looked dull and tired and sad, and she was struck with sudden pity. "Can't you store your things? Haven't you got any folks?"

He shook his head. "No, I might as well clean out." He stalked around the room, his plump hands thrust in his pockets. "I always liked it here," he said angrily. "But I'm going on tour with a band, and I can't afford to keep this place up."

Linny slipped down into a Windsor rocker. She

rocked gently, looking at the cold fireplace where Cousin Joe used to sit and chew on winter apples.

"I grew up on the East Side of New York. Now in New York you can go back after ten years and you wouldn't know the street where you were born, to say nothing of the neighbors. But here . . ." He waved his arm in a wide sweep. "I guess until the dam was built, nothing ever changed here—the mountains, the valley, the same old farmhouses and families. . . ."

Linny's eyes twinkled. "Mr. Goldstein," she said suddenly, "when you bought the Brick House, did anyone ever tell you about the man who built it, a man named Deliverance Tainter?"

"No," he said, a spark of interest lighting his eyes.

"Deliverance Tainter was my great-great-grandfather," she began.

What possessed her she didn't know. Words poured out of her, as fast as they ever poured out of Grandma. She told him about old Deliverance staggering up the road dripping wet and singing happily. She told him about Nathan coming for Betsy and mean old Caleb hogging the property and Cousin Joe and Grandpa drinking cider in the firelight while the phonograph played "I'll take another bottle of Wizard Oil."

"Now think of all that going on in this house!" Mr. Goldstein laughed until he had to take off his glasses and wipe his eyes.

The sun crept down the sky; the shadows lengthened. When at last she told him about Grandma losing the use of her leg and the old house being sold to the Power Company, he gave a little cough. They sat silent listening to the chirp of a cricket from a dark corner and the lonely wailing of the wind down the cold chimney.

She heard a clock strike and jumped to her feet. "Mercy, I must be going."

He picked up the small radio and held it out to her. "You take this to your grandfather with my compliments," he said.

She flushed with embarrassment. She couldn't take such a gift from a stranger! But there was something about the look on his face that stopped the quick protest on her tongue, and she thanked him warmly.

He patted her shoulder. "Well . . . good luck, kid," he said, his eyes kind and knowing.

"Good luck to you too," she said. She felt as if they shared something together.

When she climbed Chase Hill it was almost dark. As she turned into the yard she saw that the barn doors were bolted, and the garden was lost in shadows. She hastened across the grass, wet now with the night dew. Aunt Gloria had probably forgotten to stoke the fire, and it was supper time. The house looked bare with the rugs taken up, half the furniture gone, and the ruffled curtains down. Grandpa still sat huddled in Grandma's rocker, his white head pressed to the dark window.

His dim old eyes peered up at Linny. "Any of you folks see old Link hereabouts today?" he quavered.

Uncle Nat's face looked harassed. Gloria bit her lip. Linny bent down and took one of Grandpa's withered hands in hers.

"Grandpa, don't you remember?" she said loud and clear. "Uncle Nat talked it all over with you. The house is sold to the Power Company, and in a few days you are going down to Boston to live with Uncle Nat."

He rocked gently, brooding over her words, while three anxious faces watched him. "If Kit was here she'd bind a hunk of pork rind around my sore throat," he complained.

"I'll get you another aspirin, Pa," Gloria said.

"Grandpa, look what I've got for you." Linny set the radio in his lap.

His swollen fingers stroked the polished case. "A radio!" he said in awe. "Where'd you git it?"

"Mr. Goldstein down at the Brick House sent it to you with his compliments," she said. "He's selling out and leaving town."

He tugged at his beard. "Mr. Goldstein, eh? Well, I'll be hornswaggled!"

"We had a good visit, Grandpa. I told him all about old Deliverance. . . ." Linny rattled on.

"Gracious, Linny, you sound just like Ma," Gloria said.

Linny stoked the fire, which was almost out, and stirred up hot biscuits for supper. She fried potatoes, bacon, and eggs, and warmed up a baked Indian pudding. A heavy weight seemed to have slid away from her this afternoon, leaving her free and strong. Now she knew with a clear, bright certainty what she was going to do.

As Linny set the earthen teapot on the table her eye lighted on the blue glass toothpick holder at Grandpa's place. "Bless you, Aunt Gloria," she said as Gloria dropped wearily into a chair.

"I don't know where you get your energy from, Linny. I'm too tired to eat," Gloria said.

Uncle Nat helped Grandpa into his chair at the table. "Where have you been all afternoon, Linny?" he said.

"Down at the Brick House, Uncle Nat. I had a long walk and a chance to think. I've got some news for all of you," she said in excitement. She drew a deep breath.

"I've thought it all over, and I know what I want to do. I'm going to apply at the Memorial Hospital down in Fitchburg to train for a nurse."

Gloria's fork clattered to the floor. She seemed

shocked. "Linny! Hospitals are frightfully short-handed. They'll work you like a dog. You'll have to empty bedpans and see people die."

Linny poured another cup of tea and helped herself to more potatoes. "I saw a man die in the hurricane. Folks called him Hopping Frog. He drove the stage. I guess I can stand the sight of a little blood."

Gloria's cheeks flamed fire red. "Now don't try to tell me to save my breath, Nat. I'm not going to stand by and see Linny ruin her life. In Boston she could go to art school or college. She could have every advantage."

A sly look crept across Uncle Nat's thin, nervous face. "Have you forgotten how once you raised such a stink pining for the life cultural that your ma let you have your way and sent you down to Boston to live with your Aunt Zina?"

Gloria ruffled up her feathers like a Bantam hen. "I don't see any Vermont soil under *your* fingernails," she said tartly. "Your ma took on like a wild woman when you went, but you went just the same."

"Yep, that's the Chase of it." Uncle Nat grinned.

Now they'd squabble until the last gun was fired, Linny thought, but it didn't bother her. Calmly she buttered another biscuit. Then, suddenly, a laugh boomed up out of her, a great, hearty crow.

Grandpa raised his head from his plate, a listening look on his dimmed face. "Sake's alive, but it seems good to hear a little noise around here," he said. "Where'd you say you was goin', Linny?"

21

As LINNY LOOKED out the kitchen window, she could see the familiar hills, purplish gray. The sky was clouded over, but the maples were a blaze of glory. Soon the first snow would be falling, but there would be no path through the snow from house to barn, no smoke threading up from the chimney.

Without Grandma the house seemed deathly still. She battled against the hot tears that stung her eyelids. Grandma would be ashamed of her if she cried. She fingered Great-Grandmother Betsy's brooch at the neck of her dress and felt comforted, as if a hand had reached out to help her.

The phone rang, and Mart's calm voice came over the wire. "I'm sorry we can't get to the station to see you off, Linny. The baby's fussy. Have a good trip and don't forget us. I'll send you some molasses cookies. I've heard that girls in dormitories like something to chew on."

"Thank you, Mart, thank you for everything," Linny said, choking back the tears. "I hope you have a good winter with not too much snow."

As she hung up the receiver she felt as if she were moving in a dream. She wound her red scarf, which Grandma had knit for her, around her neck and pulled on her tweed coat. Her bag stood on the floor, packed and ready.

"Well, say, Linny, where you bound for?" Grandpa in Grandma's rocker, the red plaid blanket over his knees, seemed to have shrunk down almost as small as Cousin Joe.

"Why, Grandpa, don't you remember?" she said loudly. "I'm going to Fitchburg to learn to be a nurse."

Uncle Nat stalked into the kitchen, nervous hands thrust in his pockets. He pulled out a flutter of pink paper and held it out to her. "Here, Linny, this half of the proceeds of the house sale is for you. It's what Ma wants you to have for your education."

She glanced at the figures on Uncle Nat's check and thought of how they used to work to scrape together money, getting fifty cents for an ax handle, a dollar for berries. . . .

"You keep it, Uncle Nat," she said. "You've already given me more than enough. I can get a scholarship for my tuition and wait on table to help out with board and room."

She was grateful he didn't press her. "I'll put it in the bank for you, Linny. It may come in handy someday."

Gloria appeared in the doorway. She picked a piece of lint from Linny's coat. "Well, you look neat and clean and healthy, if not very stylish," she said with a sigh.

"At least you ought to let me run you down to the Falls," Uncle Nat fumed. He had rented a car in Wilmington to drive the family to Boston.

"Thanks just the same, Uncle Nat," Linny said. "But Jan would be disappointed. He's gone to the trouble of asking the Power Company for time off to take me to the train."

"Well, good luck, Linny." Uncle Nat hugged her warmly. "You let us know how you make out."

"Have a good trip, darling," Gloria said, and kissed Linny's cheek. "When you get to Fitchburg buy yourself a pretty dress."

Linny leaned over the rocker and laid her cheek close to Grandpa's. "Good-bye, Grandpa."

"Say, Linny, you bring me a plug of Old Honesty when you come back from the store," he quavered.

Gloria bit her lip and turned away.

Linny patted Grandpa's shoulder and fled out the door.

Jan was waiting in the yard, the motor throbbing. He stowed her suitcase and the sack of shelled beans in the back of the car and helped her into the front seat.

As they drove out of the yard she didn't look back at the tired old house drooping toward the waiting earth. But she let her eyes linger on the stiff, green, upward-reaching firs and the maples threaded with gold, on the granite rocks in the pasture bedded in bronzed fern. The air tasted like cider. Soon there would be frost.

As they rounded the bend at the foot of the hill Linny looked at the crystal-clear water that rippled over the spot where Mart's house had stood. The big square house had always looked so solid. But it was gone now as if it had never been.

Now they were rumbling by the old district school-house. That awakened memories. It seemed only the other day the children had made fun of Jan because he was a Pole. But Jan was never one to look back, Linny thought. He would bury his hurts with no complaint.

Swimming up out of the pool of her memories, Linny felt a tightening in her chest. It was impossible to think of a future without Jan in it.

He handed her a package. "Thought you could use this," he said.

A present to remember Jan by! With eager fingers she

opened the package and found a handsome box of writing paper.

"Oh, thank you, Jan. I'll write to you every week," she exclaimed.

Jan slowed down as they neared the store. Old Mose Shawn pulled up in the new bus that had replaced Hopping Frog's car, wrecked in the hurricane.

"Hi, Linny, where you bound for?" old Mose called out as he swung down the mailbags.

"I'm going to a hospital in Fitchburg to learn to be a nurse," Linny said. Saying it out loud made it somehow more real.

"Learnin' how to take care of sick folks is mighty useful," old Mose said approvingly. "Your folks'll be proud of you."

Linny got out of the car and reached for the beans. "I'm going to trade with Mr. Butterfield," she said.

Mose nodded in approval. "If you wait long enough, things come full circle," he said. "Good to have the old store back. What do you hear from your Uncle Truman?"

"We haven't heard from him in ages," Linny said, shutting the car door.

"Wal, likely you will if you wait long enough," Mose said mysteriously.

"Mose Shawn, what have you got up your sleeve?" Linny demanded.

Old Mose shook his shaggy head. "What I want to know is what did Truman Chase git out of goin' to Floridy? Settin' around hotels, and him a Yank!" He spat, reached down, and swung the mailbags over his shoulder and headed for the post office.

Following old Mose, Linny made for the door.

Jan spoke up from the car. "Don't be too long, Linny, or you'll miss your train."

As she stepped through the doorway Linny's eyes lighted on two children cowering near the counter, a girl with tight pigtails and dark, shadowed eyes and a smaller red-cheeked boy with traces of tears on his smudgy cheeks. Their neat navy sailor suits were crumpled and soiled. Mr. Butterfield was trying to bait them with a couple of lollipops.

"Never did see a young'un that wouldn't pounce on a lollipop," Mr. Butterfield complained, turning toward Linny.

"What's up?" boomed old Mose, and planted his thick legs wide apart, staring down at the small mournful faces.

"Gol durn it, they're refugee young'uns sent out by that New York Children's Committee," Mr. Butterfield wailed. "They're headed for the Wheelers, and the Wheelers is gone fer the day. Didn't expect the children till tomorrow. Must have been a hitch someplace, 'cuz instead of sending 'em to the Falls, they sent 'em to North Adams. And blamed if they wuzn't sent over here on an oil truck. Miz Wheeler she'll be fit to be tied."

Old Mose fished in his pocket and brought out some reddish crumbles. "Have some spruce gum," he bellowed, holding out his huge hand.

As the children retreated in fright, a dim memory awakened in Linny. She looked at the children, moved by some old and familiar knowing. "Mr. Butterfield," she said quickly, "why don't you phone the minister's wife?"

"By golly, why didn't I think of her afore." Mr. Butterfield hastened to the phone.

Linny turned to the children. How thin they were, the skin stretched tight over their small wrists and ankles.

"I think I was just about as big as you are the first day

I came to Sadawga Springs," she began, her voice slow and calm. "It was snowing. My, such a big snow! I thought the village was buried in snow, and I didn't see anybody I knew."

They turned dark, solemn eyes on her, wary as little foxes frightened at the stir of a leaf. The girl picked nervously at her crumpled dress. "We came on a ship," she offered, "and there were big, tall waves."

The boy twisted one of the buttons on his jacket. "There was lots of fog and the whistles kept blowing."

"But now you're *here!*" Linny's eyes sparkled. "And the air smells like snow. Do you know what fun snow is? I used to coast down two hills all the way to the village."

The boy's eyes brightened. The girl moved a step toward Linny.

"And in the spring I used to help my grandpa gather maple sap, and I'd watch it bubble in a great vat outdoors and have sugar on snow."

"Sugar on snow," the girl said in wonder.

"Tomorrow you'll think Christmas has come," Linny went on. "Mrs. Wheeler has a cat with five kittens, two hound dogs, and horses and cows and sheep."

The boy lifted up his head. "Dogs," he said wistfully. "And horses!"

"And don't think they won't be glad to see you," Linny said with hearty sureness. "Why, this whole village will be your aunts and uncles. In no time you'll have folks a-plenty. You'll see."

"Minister's wife is comin' right over," Mr. Butterfield called out. He let out a sigh of relief.

"We've got to be stepping, Linny," Jan urged from the doorway.

"I'm coming," she said, picking up the lollipops and putting them within reach of small fingers. "Here are the beans, Mr. Butterfield. Will you give the credit to the children?"

"Certain sure," he said. "Hold on a minute." He reached into the glass case. "When you was a little tyke you was always mighty fond of chocolate creams. You take a box with you to munch on the train."

Linny tucked the box under her arm and pressed his rheumatic fingers. "Good-bye, Mr. Butterfield, and thanks.

"Good-bye, children," she said, giving them a little wave of her hand. "Remember what I said."

"Good-bye," they chorused, waving back. They had picked up the lollipops and were sucking on them.

All the way to the station Linny was silent, sitting up stiffly in the car, her head swimming. A misty sun issued from the gray sky and shone wanly on stripped fields. Every mile they went seemed to take her farther away from Jan.

As if he had read her thoughts, he said, "Linny, I've got my own paycheck now. Ma lets me keep it and pay her board. You send me your telephone number, and I'll call you."

"Oh, Jan, that will be wonderful," Linny cried, her spirits lifting.

"If I can keep this old rattletrap on the road, I'll be down to see you. You know how it is with me, Linny. There's never been anyone but you ever since we were kids."

"Nothing ever separated us but the Power Company," Linny said. "I'm sorry I made such a fuss."

"Try to think of the future and not of the past," Jan said. "You've got plenty of spunk. Remember the time when every kid in school was calling me a Polack and you snapped your fingers at the whole bunch and gave me an apple?"

Linny smiled. "Times change and sometimes for the better. No Polish children today will go through what you suffered."

"I had you," Jan said.

"And I had you, Jan," Linny said softly.

He took one hand from the steering wheel and squeezed her fingers. But he took his hand back quickly when old Mose passed them, driving like a wild man.

"Mose said he had a passenger coming on the up train. I can't imagine who it could be," Linny said.

The car clattered through a covered bridge and Jan pulled up at the station.

"Jumpin' Jiminy, the up train's in, and there he be," she heard Mose say.

Linny jumped out of the car and ran with outstretched arms. "Uncle Truman!" she sobbed, flinging herself on him. "Uncle Truman Chase!"

Warmed by the Florida sun, his white mustache neatly clipped, his squat heavy figure bursting out of a good gray suit, Uncle Truman looked pert as a turkey.

"You old hoss thief!" As Linny stepped back, old Mose slapped Truman on the back.

The next few minutes flew as Uncle Truman and Linny sat in the chilly station talking the handle off a pump, as Grandma would say, Linny thought, trying to tell Uncle Truman everything at once. Her tongue clattered a mile a minute as she told him of Cousin Joe's funeral, the hurricane, Grandpa's accident, Grandma's stroke, and the house's having been sold to the Power Company.

Uncle Truman gave a deep sigh. "I can't figger Kit being helpless. Seems like there wasn't anything that could stop Kit." He twirled his hat in his hand. "How's your grandpa taking it?"

Linny bit her lip. "Grandpa says he wishes he could hear some noise."

There was a shine to Uncle Truman like the polish on a rubbed McIntosh. "What are you going to do in Sadawga Springs, Uncle Truman?"

"I aim to cut lumber and open up the old mill on Freezin' Hole." He flirted with the ends of his mustache. "I figger now's the time to come home and git down to business."

"Grandpa says there's a good market for spruce now," Linny said, surprised.

He felt in his vest pocket and came up with a dog-eared photograph. His eyes lit up.

"Ain't she as likely lookin' as ever you set eyes on? Her name's Georgia, and she's got white hair and a skin like peaches. She's a widow, hails from South Carolina. I met her in a hotel in Miami."

Linny looked at the picture, speechless. "Why, Uncle Truman!" she said weakly.

Uncle Truman chuckled. "Well, she's a Chase now. We got hitched a couple of weeks back. And did her young'uns raise Hob! They just want to keep her settin'. But she don't want to set. She wants to do."

"She's lovely, Uncle Truman," Linny said in awe. "But isn't she kind of delicate to take up on Freezin' Hole?"

"Pooh, power's on, ain't it? I aim to fix that old house up there all electric. She'll have everything to do with. Soon's I git it halfway in shape she's comin' up and finish the way she wants."

Linny stared earnestly at the gentle face. "What does Mart say?" she asked.

"I'm no hand at letter writin'. I figgered 'twould be better to tell Mart in person that I've put somebody in her ma's place."

"Mart will be glad for you, I know," Linny said stoutly. "She knows you'd never be happy living at Sophronie's. I wonder sometimes about Grandma and Grandpa being transplanted. This afternoon Nat's driving Grandpa down to Boston. Grandma's going to stay awhile at a Boston hospital."

His eyes narrowed. "They goin' to live with Nat?"

Linny nodded. "There's no place else."

He pursed his lips. "Nat's wife is kind of bossy, ain't she?"

"I don't think she'll let Grandpa have a spittoon in the parlor," said Linny.

Uncle Truman paused. "Lookin' into the future's like spittin' in the wind," he said, "but I'll do what I can. I'll have Mose drive me up right away so I can see Newt before he leaves. And I'll git down to that Boston hospital to see Kit. If Kit's leg improves I don't see why they couldn't spend next summer with us up on Freezin' Hole."

Linny dabbed at her eyes. "Bless you, Uncle Truman," she said. "God bless you." She leaned over and kissed his old apple cheek.

Old Mose and Jan appeared in the doorway. "Down train's comin' in," Mose announced.

Rocking around ledges came the narrow-gauge train toward the station, its long melancholy hoot penetrating the whole valley. Snorting and panting, it came closer, until Linny saw blobs of faces pressed to the windows.

"Linny," old Mose rose his voice above the belching of the train, "you ain't leavin' Vermont behind. You're takin' it with you." His giant hand thrust something soft and furry into her hand. "For luck," he shouted. "Maybe 'twon't do no good, and then again maybe 'twon't do no harm neither."

"Thanks, Mr. Shawn." Her fingers closed tightly around the rabbit's foot, and she tucked it into her coat pocket.

"I've got everything," Jan said, following her up the train steps. In the train he lifted her suitcase into a rack above the seat. Swooping her into his arms, he pressed his lips to hers for a brief second, and then he was gone.

A sudden wild dizziness rushed to Linny's head. She pressed her face against the window to catch a last glimpse of Jan's dark head and of the tough old faces of Mose and Uncle Truman. It seemed only yesterday that she had stepped down from the train into snow. A flurry of snow, budding green and bloom, and then snow again. Time went by like a bird on the wing.

But nothing could take away memories. . . . *Cousin Joe and Grandpa in the firelight.. . . "I'll take another bottle of Wizard oil." . . . Lantern light on the pasture hill. . . . green growing fields of corn. . . . Mart's slow, rich voice: "I always like the time when the beans come." . . . The golden mounds of Grandma's griddle cakes . . . the squeak of Grandma's rockers . . . her lusty old voice singing, "There's honey in the rock for you. . . ."*

She turned from the window, took off her coat and scarf, and sat down. The train gathered speed and fell into a steady hum. She opened the box of chocolate creams.